empower:

fight like a girl

a collection of short stories by:

Amy Berg
Cherry Chevapravatdumrong
Akela Cooper
Liz Edwards
Jane Espenson
Shalisha Francis & Nadine Knight
Lisa Klink
Pang-Ni Landrum

Lauren LeFranc
Kam Miller
Jess Pineda
Jennifer Quintenz
Lisa Randolph
Kay Reindl
Kira Snyder
Jeane Wong

Word's Empower
MEDIA

*Dedicated to Maurissa, all the unsung heroes battling lupus,
and the loved ones supporting them in this fight.*

contents

Acknowledgments   vii
"Outlaw" by Amy Berg   1
"Healthy Happy Hailie!" by Cherry Chevapravatdumrong   9
"Hallelujah" by Akela Cooper   21
"Three Minutes" by Liz Edwards   37
"INT. WOLF—NIGHT" by Jane Espenson   45
"XAYMACA" by Shalisha Francis & Nadine Knight   51
"Collapse" by Lisa Klink   61
"Suzie Homemaker Apocalypse Ass Kicker" by Pang-Ni Landrum   71
"Positive Symptoms" by Lauren LeFranc   83
"Dangerous Stars" by Kam Miller   93
"Home" by Jess Pineda   113
"Stolen Child" (a *Daughters of Lilith* story) by Jennifer Quintenz   125
"Still Waters" by Lisa Randolph   145
"Martyoshka" by Kay Reindl   161
"Bat Girl" by Kira Snyder   175
"Crystal Brook" by Jeane Wong   183
About the Lupus Foundation of America, Inc.   191
A Note From The Authors   193

acknowledgements

When we set out to organize this project, we knew it would hinge on the support of a community of writers—without whom we would have no book. The enthusiastic response to our initial inquiry overwhelmed and touched us. These generous women took time away from busy lives, development and production schedules, and their families to share their talents with us. Our sincerest gratitude goes out to each and every writer who contributed a story to help make this anthology into a stronger weapon in the fight against lupus.

We are also indebted to two editors, Julie Van Keuren and Lisa Benjamin Goodgame, who generously donated their time and expertise to go over every story for this volume.

Special thanks to Sophie Yan at the Lupus Foundation of America, Inc., whose support has been invaluable throughout this process.

To our own families, we couldn't have put this together without your encouragement and mad kid-watching skills.

And, of course, to Maurissa Tancharoen Whedon whose remarkable strength and unflagging spirit inspired the entire idea behind this collection... stories about strong, badass women, written by strong, badass women, in honor of a strong, badass woman.

- Pang-Ni Landrum & Jennifer Quintenz

"Outlaw"
by Amy Berg

T he only glimpse he caught was a dress in the wind. The marshal leaned out of the car for a better look. It was exactly what he thought he saw: a woman in full sprint, her buxom bosom bouncing wildly with each step, kicking up dirt with her boots.

"Slow down!" he shouted at the conductor, keeping one eye on the woman.

The train had just left Charleston, bound for the West with a freight of settlers embarking on new beginnings. Apparently one of them was a little late getting started.

She caught up to the train even before it slowed, throwing a suitcase past the outstretched hand of the marshal, who grabbed her and pulled her inside.

"Cutting it a little close, aren't—" he started, unable to finish. Seconds after planting her feet, she smacked him upside the head with the suitcase. Already half-out the door, the blow carried him the rest of the way. She grabbed his revolver from its holster as he fell, then watched as he landed hard in the dirt just outside the tracks.

She dusted herself off, then dumped out a handful of rocks from the otherwise-empty suitcase. She held it open as she walked down the aisle past wide-eyed passengers.

"No one needs to get hurt," she said with disturbing grace. "But in case you get any ideas, you should know I ain't no stranger to killin'."

As she passed, billfolds, pocket watches, and other valuables were tossed into the case. A moment's hesitation was greeted with a pistol whip.

At the end of the car was a door to the engine compartment. She didn't bother to knock.

The conductor turned to find a revolver a few centimeters from his face. He stepped aside, allowing the woman to pull the brake lever.

The screeching sound was deafening. The conductor clutched his ears and peered through the window. A hundred yards up the tracks, where the train would come to a stop, was a horse tied to a tree.

"Thanks for the ride," Josey told him. "But I'll be getting off here."

The excavation started five paces past the cactus to the west of the trail. Ridley paused to remove his hat, using his sleeve to wipe beads of sweat from his brow. He glanced around nervously, anticipating unwanted company. His instincts were correct.

Across the trail were two unseen observers masked by the cover of night.

"You were right," Josey said to her partner. "He led us right to it."

In the distance, Ridley hit something with his shovel. He reached down to brush aside loose dirt, revealing a metal box. He peeled off the lid and smiled. It was all there. Stacks of $5 bank notes and dozens of silver coins. This wasn't someone's personal savings buried out in the middle of a prairie; this was a criminal haul.

"What now?" Josey asked.

"We set the trap," her partner replied. "Go 'round and come up his backside ... surprise him."

Josie nodded, disappearing into the dark as her partner stepped out into the open.

He pulled his revolver from its holster and carefully approached the scene.

"It's over, Ridley," he shouted. "I'm taking you in."

A gunshot rang out. The two men stared at each other until one of them dropped. Ridley, unarmed and unharmed, remained on his feet.

In front of him stood Josey, a trigger at her fingertips.

"What the hell?!" he exclaimed, recognizing her in his final moments.

After dispensing with him, Josey picked up the metal box, wiping away blood from its lid. She opened it, smiled, then walked away, pausing over her partner's body.

"Thanks for the tip, Mr. Pinkerton."

♦ ❖ ♦

The tea leaves spit out like chewed tobacco. The soothsayer stared into the bowl, illuminated by candlelight, analyzing the messages within. Suddenly she recoiled, her silk shawl receding enough to expose the shock in her eyes.

"What is it?" the client asked, jumping to his feet.

"I—I can't say," she replied.

"I'm paying you to say!" he shouted. His attention was quickly diverted to the sudden scrambling of footsteps just outside the door.

"It's okay," the soothsayer assured the source of the scurrying before turning back to her client. "I don't believe in violence," she said. "But I can't speak for my associates."

"Please," the man pleaded, "I need to know."

Tom Ridley was a businessman with the countenance of a gunslinger. Normally he was in control of his emotions, but not on this day.

"I've seen this configuration before," said the soothsayer. "I've seen it exactly, in fact. Not two days ago. A woman was here, concerned her husband was unfaithful."

Ridley paced behind her, listening intently but saying nothing.

"Your wife," the soothsayer offered. "Did she tell you about our reading?"

"Never mind that," he replied. "What did you say to her?"

"This pattern here is the goat," she said, indicating a collection of leaves near the base of the bowl. "It symbolizes betrayal, but not in affairs of the heart. Have you reason to suspect an associate has deceived you?"

"That lying bastard," Ridley grumbled, slamming his fist on the table so hard it overturned the bowl. He tossed two coins on the table and stormed out.

Moments after his exit, another man entered. The soothsayer stood up from the table to greet Mr. Pinkerton, yanking the shawl from her head.

"How'd I do?" she asked.

"Very well, Miss Wales," he said. "So well you're starting to make me nervous."

3

She removed her robe, revealing a collared shirt over dirty corduroys. Pinkerton handed her a gun belt with a shiny new Colt .45 in its holster. She smiled, admiring it.

"You earned this," he said.

"Do I keep following the woman?"

"She's done her job," Pinkerton replied. "Now it's his turn."

◆ ❖ ◆

The man paced in front of the cell, keys jangling from his belt next to the revolver nestled tightly in its holster. "Not gonna lie," he sighed. "You're a hard one to find."

"Wasn't trying to make it easy," came the reply from the shadows.

"I'd like to know how you found him."

The prisoner spoke with an uneasy calm. "Same way you found me, I reckon."

He expected resistance, but not an opportunity to gloat. "My men tracked him for weeks but were always a day behind."

"You need better men," the prisoner responded. She stepped into the light, her dress soiled from days of trudging through mud. Her skin, overexposed to the elements, pink and peeling. She ran a hand through her hair as if that'd make her suddenly presentable.

"Hardin's a coldblooded killer," she said. "You may've paid your men well enough to find him, but to bring him in? That's a price even you can't afford."

"Who is it you think I am, Miss Wales?"

"I know you ain't no lawman," she replied.

She nodded at his revolver. "Barrel's got years of rust, but the handle's still smooth," she noted. "And your holster's too far back for a quick pull."

He glanced down at his belt. She wasn't wrong. About any of it. "Don't need to start a fight if you can win an argument," he offered.

"So you just talked the sheriff into giving you them keys?"

"I'm a recruiter," he explained. "I work for the Pinkertons."

"The guys who sort it out when the law can't."

"That's right," he said plainly. "So I guess you figured out why I'm here."

She nodded. "You need better men."

4

He smelled like whisky and horseshit. Every inch of James Hardin made her want to vomit, but he was too drunk to interpret her grimace as anything but seductive. His dry, calloused hands ripped at her skin as he ran them up the back of her legs.

"I'm Josey," she offered, nervously licking her lips as she straddled him in the chair, her too-tight dress hiked up to her waist.

Hardin pulled off his Stetson, revealing sparse strings of hair glued to his scalp by sweat. He offered a crooked smile, placing the dirt-stained hat atop her finely coiffed hair. "We goin' for a ride, Josey?"

She gently coaxed him out of the chair, leading him past the crowded bar, the tuneless upright, and the other whores gunning for marks. As they ascended the rickety staircase, Hardin glanced back at his men, their thick beards soaking up much of the liquor their mouths couldn't manage to haul in.

"Don't wait up, boys," he slurred, before disappearing down a narrow hallway.

Josey's hands shook as she unlocked the door to a back room, allowing him to stumble inside. By all appearances, this was her first time.

Hardin crudely bounced on the cot, testing its rigidity. "You scared of me?" he asked.

"Used to be," she replied, steeling her nerves. "But I ain't no more." Hardin's eyes narrowed, scrambling for recognition, then widened just as suddenly.

"Well, shit."

Downstairs, the music drowned out most conversation, let alone the thud of a body hitting the floorboards above. The only evidence was the small puff of dust between two beams and the slow drip of blood through a knothole.

"Third time this week," said the old man, staring at the hole in the barbed-wire fence. "We lost a half-dozen already." He turned to his grandson. "Hand me those pliers."

Luke was only ten, but already an experienced farmhand. He was ready with whatever tools his pops might need. "Maybe they're biting through it?"

"Cows are dumb," the old man replied. "But they ain't stupid." He pointed to the section of wire around the hole. "See how clean the edges are? If I had to guess—"

The lesson was interrupted by the sound of galloping horses drawing near. The hairs on the old man's neck stood up.

"Take your sister back to the house," he urged. Luke, confused, glanced at his younger sister picking daisies near the herd. Hesitation was his first mistake.

"Need some help?" shouted the lead rider as the group pulled up alongside the fence.

The old man shook his head. "Thank you kindly, but no."

"You sure?" the rider replied with a spine-chilling smile. "Looks to me like you got a poacher on your hands." He studied the old man closely, following his gaze to the rifle leaning against the fence ten feet away and then to his grandchildren. Both men knew this would only end one way.

"Let the kids go," the old man pleaded. "You can have the cattle."

"I'll have 'em either way."

The old man took one square to the chest. He stutter-stepped for a moment before falling to his knees.

Luke went for the rifle. That was his second mistake. He was already bleeding profusely by the time his sister reached his side. She pressed her hands against his stomach.

"What's your name, girl?" asked the ringleader, stepping down from his horse.

"Josey," she said, trembling, a small puddle forming near her feet as he approached. "You gonna kill me?"

"No," he replied, kneeling in front of her. "Know why?"

Josie shook her head. The man leaned in. He swept a lock of hair away from her face.

"'Cause if you kill everybody," he explained, "ain't no one left to fear you."

About The Author

Amy Berg is a writer/producer/geek hyphenate. She's written for numerous television shows including *Person of Interest* (CBS), *Eureka* (Syfy), *Leverage* (TNT), and *The 4400* (USA) and is the creator of the popular digital series, *Caper*. She's currently attached to several television and feature film projects she can't yet name lest she lose contact with vital appendages. Aside from lending her awkward public speaking skills to such geektastic ventures as w00tstock, you can occasionally find her on the convention circuit shilling shows. Berg has scripted kiddie comedy, soap operas, period pieces, crime dramas, science fiction and has also dabbled in comic books. She plainly needs to focus.

Follow her on Twitter: @bergopolis
Watch "Caper" on Hulu: www.hulu.com/caper

"Healthy Happy Hailie!"
by Cherry Chevapravatdumrong

HEALTHY HAPPY HAILIE!
a food, fun & fitness blog!

HOME ABOUT ME FAQ RECIPES & WORKOUTS LINKS I LOVE! CONTACT

October 8, 2013

You guys, I'm gonna cut and paste my "About Me" section here because it's hilarious. What was I thinking? How dumb was I back then? Read this. Even if you have already, read it again, because I just did and I basically want to kill myself:

ABOUT ME

Hi, I'm Hailie, and welcome to my blog! This is where I post my favorite recipes, fitness tips, and also just write about the general craziness that is my life! I used to be an actress, but now I blog full time, and it truly is a rewarding career. I eat paleo, I stay active, and I try my best to be healthy and happy! Come share my journey!

I mean…right? What was I doing, injecting 100% pure sunshine into my veins? Because if I'd been telling the truth, it would've gone a little something more like this:

ABOUT ME

Here's what you think is going to happen when you, the prettiest girl at your high school (as voted by your 1,800 fellow students)

9

three years running (freshman year you hadn't grown boobs yet), put all your belongings in a car and drive from West Bloomfield, MI to Los Angeles, CA:

1. Arrive
2. Become movie star

Here's what actually happens:

1. Arrive
2. Rejection
3. Rejection
4. Rejection
5. Starvation because everybody here is super thin and therefore if you starve you will no longer have to deal with rejection
6. Rejection
7. Starvation because you literally ran out of money to buy food
8. Rejection
9. Rejection
10. Fuck this, I'm trying a different line of work

See, that's the truth. That's the actual truth right there. I *am* healthy and happy, and I *do* love this blog, and I *do* welcome you to it, but I left a lot out before. Like the eating disorder (and subsequent recovery…although, frankly, I still take it day by day, so I'm hesitant to say I'm fully out of the woods). And the part where my boyfriend at the time dumped me for a girl who'd just gotten a (tiny, by the way) role in a miniseries and weighed fourteen pounds less than me while being three inches taller. That was years ago; I'm over it. OVER IT! I'm just telling you guys now because I'm a little loopy from anesthesia (got my wisdom teeth out—all four of them, this morning, all at once) and I just woke up from my post-surgery nap, and it's dark outside, and I haven't checked the time because I'm in too much pain, and my mouth is stuffed with bloody gauze, and it's gross, and I probably shouldn't even post this. Whatever. I'm gonna take, like, six Vicodin and then post this. Hahahahha who cares aaaaa!!!!! POSTING! I'm gonna regret this tomorrow, probably. Sorry. POSTING!

October 9, 2013

Hi everyone! I'm so sorry for yesterday! I had just gotten oral surgery and was clearly high as a kite. I even contemplated taking that post down, but I've decided to leave it up instead, as a lesson to myself, and to others, that all surgery is serious. Anesthesia can absolutely affect your health, so if you ever undergo a procedure where it's necessary, make sure to take care of yourself both before and afterwards. Anyway, back to our regularly scheduled programming:

No workout today because I'm still recovering (giving myself three full days until I hit the gym again, although I may do some bodyweight exercises at home tomorrow, depending on how I feel).

Today's paleo eats: nothing for breakfast, nothing for lunch, nothing for dinner (my mouth still hurts so I didn't want to attempt even soup). I did drink a lot of water, though, and a little bit of kombucha. Water and kombucha are the best!

Stay healthy! Stay happy! :)

October 10, 2013

Feeling so much better today! I refuse to be kept down by the holes in my mouth formerly known as my wisdom teeth. Actually, I *am* too tired to blog much (not being able to eat = zero energy), but I just wanted to check in and let everyone know that I'm okay. Have any of you ever gotten your wisdom teeth out? Let me know in the comments section!

Stay healthy! Stay happy! :)

October 12, 2013

I would post a picture of my breakfast this morning except I didn't really eat any. I made a smoothie (frozen banana + spinach + strawberries + almond butter + chia seeds = soooo good!) and like any good blogger, I took a photo of it arranged on my favorite vintage silver tray with a fresh daisy and this cute little striped paper straw. It looked SO CUTE! So cute that I then tried to drink it through the straw, forgetting that the dentist told me not to use straws because the suction can sometimes mess up your stitches. One giant mouthful of salty redness later...yeah, exactly. I'll spare you further details. Let's just say the smoothie didn't go down the hatch, but a bunch of blood did. Ewww, I know.

Oddly, I feel much better now, even though I haven't eaten in days. Like, super energetic.

Stay healthy & happy! :)

October 15, 2013

This is so weird I just have to tell someone (so everyone, I guess...hi, internet!). I went in so Dr. Forrester could redo my stitches, and during the process...I could feel it. They didn't knock me out this time, just injected some local anesthesia, but it must not have worked because I could feel everything she was doing. And it hurt, but it didn't *hurt*. It didn't bother me. Pain normally really bothers me! I'll push through it during a workout, of course, but I know my limits and I always stop if it seems like it might be something serious. You can tell when your body is just complaining about one more pushup, as opposed to suffering for real. And today was real pain! But I was just like eh, whatever.

Today's workout: nothing. I'm actually beginning to feel really guilty about it—if a fitness blogger doesn't stay fit, does that mean she can still blog or is she just a FAT USELESS LUMP? Whoa, sorry. Falling back into old habits there.

Today's paleo eats: nothing. Whatever blood I accidentally swallowed during the re-stitching, I guess. Gross. Sorry.

October 23, 2013

I know. I've been AWOL. After being really honest with myself, I thought it would be best to just lay low and really recover before blogging again; I started this because it was fun, not because I felt like I needed to. But I finally worked out today! Nothing special: 100 squats, 100 pushups, 5 one-minute planks, and a few minutes of hill sprints. Today's paleo eats (or just look at the photo I posted): bone broth, green smoothie, and a few (okay, several) (okay, most of the jar) spoonfuls of homemade coconut butter. Shut up! I'm still scared to chew! Last time I tried, a few days ago, my stitches opened up again. Just a little bleeding this time, but basically it made me not want to even bother. Blood in mouth = not hungry.

Stay healthy! Stay happy! :)

October 25, 2013

Today's workout: an hour of beach running and then half an hour of the Santa Monica stairs. I wasn't even tired. I barely broke a sweat! It's weird, I never jumped on the juice cleanse bandwagon before, but maybe there *is* something to taking a break from solid food? They say it lets your body take the focus off digestion and spend time healing other things instead? Because I had INSANE energy today. And the only thing I ate was one nibble of a cacao almond protein bar. Shout out to Vixen LifeBars, by the way, for sending that box of samples! Their slogan is "Badass fuel for badass women," but that didn't stop my CrossFit buddy Jason from snarfing six. If you'd like some for yourself, check out their website and use the code "HHHBLOG" to get 20% off until midnight tomorrow! I love to hook my readers up!

Stay healthy & happy! :)

October 26, 2013

My gums are 100% healed! I feel so much better: went to the gym and lifted, took two yoga classes, and took Pip-Pip out for an hourlong hike. Unfortunately, he found a dead squirrel and had it in his mouth and I didn't even see it until he'd already brought it inside. Gross! I took a picture for you. I know I usually only post pics of my meals, but hey, a squirrel is technically a paleo eat. I'm kidding, of course—not about the paleo—it's totally paleo—but of course I didn't eat it. Though I did get a little of its blood on my hand while I was throwing it out and I screamed when it happened and then my hair fell in my face so I moved the hair and that got some blood on my face near my mouth and some of the blood ended up going in my mouth. Aaaa, disgusting!

It actually wasn't that disgusting.

I shouldn't post this. I'm going to, though, and if you don't like it, nobody's asking you to read my blog! Just point that browser somewhere else and mind your business!

Stay healthy! Stay happy! :)

November 2, 2013

So weird: I was just out walking Pip-Pip and I ran into my old commercial agent. Haven't seen her in years! Ever since she dropped me. She said I looked great, which, duh, I do! Much better than when I was her client and anorexic. It's my new diet. Which is still paleo! All parts of the animal are! Shout-out to the artisanal butcher in Los Feliz who's been hooking me up.

EDITED TO ADD: I'm seeing a lot of haters in the comments who are telling me that I am overdosing on my pain meds (not true…the Vicodin ran out a week ago) or think I am suffering from some sort of psychotic break. Wrong. I feel better than I ever have. Comments will be disabled from now on. I'm sorry to my LOYAL readers; if you have POSITIVE things to say, feel free to tweet me!

Stay healthy & happy! :)

November 5, 2013

OMG. I was out walking Pip-Pip late last night because he was freaking out and kept pawing at the door (I normally try not to go out too late by myself since he's not exactly an attack dog), and this guy comes running up to me and I was so fucking scared I hit him before he could even say anything (thanks, Krav Maga classes, I guess!) but he wasn't even mad. In FACT, he's a manager, and he said, and I quote, that I just had a certain something that drew his eye across the street to me, even though it was dark out and he could barely see. He could just sense my energy and he couldn't stop looking at me and he just had to come over. Ha! I wasn't even doing anything! I was walking my dog in SWEATPANTS. And then when I hit him, he realized I was so feisty that he just HAD to sign me. "Are you an actress? I don't even care if you aren't, I'll make you one." I told him no, that I haven't acted in years, but I also took his card. I know. It's been forever! I can't get back into the game now, can I?

November 26, 2013

I guess I can! Booked three commercials already. Barely even two weeks since I started auditioning again. And the best part is: I've lost weight. But gained muscle. And haven't even been working out. I swear. I haven't worked out in FOREVER but do you know how long I can hold a plank now? Twelve minutes. Insane, right? Without even trying. I could just hang out on my elbows and toes all day if I wanted. You could use me as a coffee table. Ha!

December 14, 2013

Confidential to the fucked-up motherfucker who roofied my drink and then offered me a ride home from the Christmas party and then tried to force your way into my house even though I said I'm tired and goodnight: It was super fun punching you multiple times in the head while wearing this gorgeous cocktail ring, it was super fun watching all your wounds bleed profusely as you lay unconscious on my doorstep, it was super fun licking the blood off your face, and congratulations, I didn't call the cops on you. I'd be mad at my manager for even inviting you to his party, but it's not his fault his friend was a secret scumbag. Besides, he introduced me to like a zillion casting directors, and they ALL loved me. I know they did. I could feel it. I literally felt like I was looking in their eyes and crawling into their brains and being wrapped up in giant warm blankets made of love and future roles on award-winning cable dramas.

December 16, 2013

Okay, fucked-up motherfucker, apparently YOU called the cops on ME. I gotta admit, I was scared when they knocked on my door. An assault charge, you say? Not after I charmed the police officer and made the whole thing go away. Oh yeah. It pays to be fit and pretty in Hollywood, I will tell you that, which obviously we all already knew. I looked that cop in the eye, said I had no idea what he was talking about, and after a moment of blankly staring at me, he agreed and left. Ta-da!

December 17, 2013

I walked into an audition today, and before I even said anything, they just gave me the part. Is that weird?

Shout-out to my pal at the UCLA platelet research center who's been hooking me up.

December 25, 2013

Pip-Pip growled at me for no reason, and then he bit me. WTF? So I bit him back. Dogs are property, so this isn't a crime. Right? Whatever. Come at me, cops. Merry Christmas.

January 5, 2014

Check out my Instagram before and after pics! From last fall, to today…it's only been three months, but I'm stronger now than I've ever been. Faster now. Obviously we knew that being fit was 80% nutrition, or even 90%, with working out being important but not necessarily the thing you should concentrate on first; that's why I tried so many different diets (vegetarian, vegan, just plain clean eating, etc.) before landing on paleo. But now that I've found this new thing, I don't even work out any more and yet I keep getting stronger (and…let's face it…better-looking). My body is sick—look at those abs!

January 9, 2014

Shout-out to the homeless guy who decided to say something incredibly crass, offensive, and unrepeatable even though I had just given you all of my change: I know you were probably mentally ill but that just means I put you out of your misery, right? And this morning I can suddenly deadlift 684 pounds. Pretty cool.

I have a confession: I may discontinue this blog soon. Acting is really picking up and I'm just kind of busy lately. Or I may just take a break, or blog less; I'm not sure. Have any of you other bloggers ever felt like quitting? Let me know in the comments! (I've enabled them again. I'm not worried about spam or negativity because I can just sort of…*think* now that I don't want that stuff to appear…and it doesn't. That sounds crazy, I know, OR DOES IT? Manifest your dreams!)

Stay healthy! Stay happy! :)

January 17, 2014

Giant, huge, big, awesome news! Can't talk about it yet. Aaaaaaaa!!!!!

January 27, 2014

Okay, the press release is out so I can finally talk (I think I could have before, actually, and if anyone had gotten mad at me, let's just say they wouldn't have stayed mad) but…I got cast in a CW pilot! And I know some of you heard already because of all the congratulatory tweets/comments you've been throwing my way, and I'm so grateful for all of them, and I want to thank you all so much! And now the world can know! I'll be playing a high school sophomore. HA, right?

Playing a teenager at my age? I literally failed and quit the business, and now I'm back and playing a KID! But that's how young I look. That's how *great* I look. I'm finally confident enough to say that, by the way. I was always my own harshest critic before, but not anymore, and never again. Because why would I criticize perfection? I look great! I'm perfect. We are *all* perfect!

The show hasn't been picked up yet, but it will be. Get me in a room with the network execs, let me look them in the eyes…it will be. If I'm still blogging by May, I will tell you *all* about the upfronts parties! They still have those, right? I don't even know anymore, I've been out of the game so long, but I'm back. I AM TOTALLY BACK AND BETTER THAN EVER!

Shout-out to my manager, who was so rude to disagree with me about whether or not I should change my hair color, but that just gave me an excuse to do what I did. You always loved Runyon Canyon, no reason you (well, most of you) shouldn't stay there forever. And now I can sprint a 48-second mile! And lift a trailer! I'm serious, I tried it when I was at Paramount the other day. Next year when I'm filming a movie (I know this will happen), I'll be able to move my trailer around with my bare hands if I feel like it. Hell, by then I'll probably be able to move it with my brain.

Stay healthy! Stay happy! Stay strong! Stay beautiful!

Forever! :)

About The Author

Cherry Chevapravatdumrong is originally from Ann Arbor, Michigan. She is the author of two novels, *She's So Money* and *DupliKate*, and a contributor to the anthology *Open Mic: Riffs on Life Between Cultures in Ten Voices*. Cherry currently serves as a writer/producer on the Fox animated series *Family Guy*. She lives in Los Angeles.

Follow her on Twitter: @cherrycheva
Follow her on Tumblr: cherrycheva.Tumblr.com
Visit her website at: www.cherrycheva.com

"Hallelujah"
by Akela Cooper

Mary kept her head to the floor as the leather belt struck her brown skin. That last hit was going to leave a horrible bruise—black, blue or purple. A few more licks and he should be finished. He was really mad at her tonight, putting his back into his punishment. He had torn her Sunday dress at the back; her mother was going to have to fix it. There was yet another hit coming. She tightened her position into a ball, tucking her head into her knees now. Biting her lip she tasted cold blood. She would not give him the satisfaction of screaming.

She was more powerful than that.

The belt struck the small of her back and she flinched. Her muscles were still aching from her trip in the forest last night. Or as her father called it while he preached "fornicating with sin". It wasn't fair; she was just practicing her religious beliefs. He didn't know any better than she did. He was as much a heathen to her as she was to him.

Her mother stood, keeping watch in the kitchen doorway. She didn't want the other children to see—or for Mary to run.

The final blow came to her shoulder blade. The skin raised and in mere moments went from red to black. Mary raised her head in defiance. She met her father's eyes.

"Are you finished, Father?"

"Only if you'll swear child, that I won't catch you doing your… your *voodoo*, any more!"

She liked it when he said "voodoo". He said it with the distaste of a white man. And that's what he was turning into: a white man wrapped in black skin.

"No, Father, you will not catch me again."

He wasn't satisfied. The same as his white people were never satisfied. Raping and pillaging whatever they found. They were never pleased. Even though he had just beaten her, even though he would do it again, she felt sorry for him. He was assimilating himself into a culture that wanted nothing to do with him. A culture that would rather see him hanged than see him succeed.

"Why not?"

She gave the expected reply: "Because we are no longer in Africa, we have become civilized, we have been Saved. Voodoo is a tool of Lucifer."

"You're coming to church," he hissed.

As Mary stood the joints and muscles in her body screamed for vengeance. She kept her eyes down, acting more subservient than Eve. If she hadn't, he probably would have seen the devil himself staring back at him through her eyes.

"You said you wouldn't do it again last week. This time I want you to promise in the name of our Lord. Promise Him you won't shame this family anymore."

She sucked in her teeth. Her mother stood erect, as if expecting a fight. It wasn't worth it. She didn't believe in it. It was meaningless to her. So she promised. But her father persisted.

"I want you to praise the Savior, praise Him and say 'Hallelujah,'" he ordered.

Mary flinched. He knew how she felt about that word. Her utter hatred of it would make the devil himself cower. It made her blood burn at the sound of him saying it. The word was so false to her, so, *enslaving*. Something inside her told her that word was a hideous lie.

"Say it," he repeated through clenched teeth, raising the belt again. "Say it or I'll start again till you do."

Her mouth went dry before she could move her tongue.

"Praise Jesus. Hallelujah."

It was like rubbing sandpaper over concrete. Both her parents flinched when she spoke. It was almost as if it wasn't her voice.

"I need to tend to my dress, Father," she said quickly, in a feminine tone she had to force from her barren mouth.

He held the belt ready to smack her again. Glancing to his wife for support, she shook her head nervously. They didn't want to make a bigger scene. The other children were scared enough.

Her mother gasped when she saw Mary's back. It was gruesome. The spots were already starting to swell and she would have to tend to them every day with cocoa butter.

Mary's father gave his consent that she stay behind under the provision that she be at church in twenty minutes—one minute more and he'd take the belt to her again. As Mary's mother tried to hand her the sewing kit her hand grazed her daughters. Through the touch, Mary could hear her mother's thoughts.

"You're supposed to set an example. Why do you resist so much? Why do you keep hurting yourself?"

Under her breath, in a hissing tone Mary replied to her mother. *"I will not be a slave to a god that doesn't exist, or a religion created by people who hate us. I will not bow to a people who forced Jesus in the heart of the Negro."*

Her mother quickly pulled away, small tears forming in her eyes. "Make sure you're at church on time," was all she said.

When the other six children were fixed in their Baptist best, Father lit the lamp and then brought the buggy around. They were having a special church service tonight. Mary didn't understand what it was about; her father had kept his mouth shut about the details. But she knew it probably had something to do with joining Mr. Petry and his new church called House of Eden. Mr. Petry was a rogue white man in a Southern Baptist community, who may be giving a co-sermon. If her father could get the white congregants to worship with the black folks, that would be history making—not to mention profitable: and white men liked having lots of money.

Mary didn't understand why her father was willing to sell out the message he was trying to preach. Supposedly Jesus didn't care about money, or having massive churches in his name. That's at least what Mary had understood of it. Of course that had come from her father's mouth, so it could very well be a lie too. He wouldn't let her read the Bible for herself. That's when she'd labeled him the heathen. He was in it for the money, not the supposed glory of his god.

She remembered the day when her father tried to baptize her. The water had started boiling as soon as she touched the holy wetness. It had scared everyone in the church. Her mother began to wither away after that, believing she had given birth to something not of Him. From that day forward she had been ostracized. Her father refused to have a "demon heathen" in his house. If she was from Satan, then she would be baptized regardless. He had her secretly done over. But as before, the water boiled. She had burns on her skin until she turned ten.

That was when she discovered how to make them go away.

She fixed the sewing needle and then retired to her room. He wouldn't get the satisfaction of seeing her undress.

"Twenty minutes!"

She heard the door slam shut. She took off her dress and sat on the bed she shared with her two other sisters. It wouldn't be long now. She began sewing the seams back together when, with acute hearing, she heard his footsteps. She pulled the dress over her bosom. Just to be spiteful, she started humming and tapping her foot.

Her father burst in an instant later.

The expression on his face, when he recognized the tune of "Wade in the Water" turned from disdain to frustration.

He'd wanted to beat her again. She kept humming and tapping her foot without missing a stitch. "I hope we sing this tonight," she lied. "It's my favorite."

His lips pulled all the way down to his chin in a frown. He didn't believe her any more than she believed the Teachings. He had to know somewhere deep in his heart that Jesus couldn't save them. They had to save themselves. He slammed the door without a word and this time he actually left. She kept sewing on her dress.

When she knew he was gone, she crawled under the bed and pulled up the center floorboard. Pulling out a jar she returned to the top of the bed. She discarded her dress. She wasn't going. She removed her underclothes and lay down naked. She examined the fluid in the jar. It was an odd recipe, but it worked. She had taken some of her monthly blood, wild red berries, fat from a neighbor's cat, zinc, butter, and semen that had been preserved in her mouth after a late-night rendezvous, mixed them into a nice paste and said a recitation. With it she repaired her bruised skin. Rubbing it on, she felt it working immediately. She went ahead and rubbed it on her whole body so her skin tone would be consistent. The darker of the black welts needed a little more, but after fifteen minutes, you couldn't tell she'd been whipped at all.

She kept herself there, knowing that her family would stay at church for the whole two hours, perhaps more, not wanting to draw attention.

Even her father wouldn't leave in the middle of his sermon. She had enough of her paste so he could beat her till his hands bled: it wouldn't change a damn thing.

She crept back under the bed, taking care to put the jar back so she wouldn't forget it. The last time she'd left one of her jars out, her little brother had found it. Her father had broken her wrist over that one.

Nothing meditation mixed with sulfur didn't fix.

She didn't know how long she'd slept, only that she woke up with her Book in her hands. She didn't remember waking up to get it. It had been hidden behind the chifforobe, in a hole that she'd carved out. She hated to think that her guard was so down that her father could catch her with the Book and burn it.

If it could be burned.

Mary rubbed the sleep out of her eyes and stretched her tired joints. She wondered what else she'd done. As she tried to sit upright, razor-sharp, piercing pains shot to her brain. She dropped her book and flopped back down on her broken mattress. She hadn't had a headache like this in years. She lay still for a few minutes smelling the fresh night air.

Until the night wind brought the smell of burning flesh. Somehow, the smell was all too familiar. Because it wasn't just any flesh. It was *human* flesh. Cooking in the night as if the Demon Gods were having a barbecue. The smell was faint at first, enough to make her mouth water. Then it overtook her senses and she gagged herself awake.

Somewhere, *someone* was on fire. It was a mass searing of flesh that tainted the night sky.

She sat up, her head throbbing. She was still naked, yet she didn't bother to cover herself. She walked straight through her house, under the eyes of the Lord, and went to her front door and snuck out onto the porch. She could see the flames from her house.

The church was burning.

Even from this distance, she could hear the sound of people screaming, and hooves pounding in erratic rhythms.

The Klan.

She immediately knew what was happening. They'd found the Nigger's Den as white folks in town called it. White Christians refused to acknowledge their black counterparts. It had to be one of them who alerted the men in white sheets. Perhaps even Mr. Petry himself. Her family had been betrayed. Though she liked the idea of her father dying, she did care about her mother and siblings.

"*Enough.*" The word slithered from her lips as she turned back to her room.

The Book was where she'd dropped it. It scared her to pick it up but there was something deep inside crying out, forcing her to.

As soon as she touched it again she knew what she must do. She was going to call it tonight. God damn this hiding. Tonight she would make the white folks pay.

And she would make her father pay. Tonight he would bow to her like he bowed to that absent God of his.

The church had already collapsed in on itself when she arrived. Her bare feet hurt from running through the woods, but her adrenaline was pumping enough for her task. She paused at the edge of the clearing and watched.

White specks moved in and out of her sight.

Yes, it was the Klan. Six of them in white sheets on coated horses. They tromped around yelling and cursing in their "victory" Two were already making nooses.

Not too many members of the congregation had escaped the roof. Those who had were sure to be hanged.

Mary felt her heritage spreading in her blood like the fire that was eating the church. The Book had belonged to her grandmother. It was time she finally used it in the open.

Her grandmother had known that it was useless, her father trying to make her a Christian. She hadn't told her son the truth about his first-born daughter, but there was nothing he could have done anyway. Baptized or not she was what she was sold as, which was not a slave. At least, not an earthly one. Her grandmother knew that within her resided the darkest family lineage that this world would ever see. Evil, original evil, was embedded in her genes. It had been riding the wave of DNA until it found a good host. After her baptism by fire, her grandmother knew which child had gotten what their African ancestors had called "Arsanduolai" The Demon of the Dead. The host had been bargained to be the first-born female. That host would be Mary until she had a daughter and so on it would go.

Mary remembered when her grandmother told her what she was.

'It's in ya, chile, ain't nuttin ya can do 'bout it. You the first afta me and you belong to The Demon. He done gone and got himself inside ya. But he ain't like no tick or no chigger naw, no, scratching, peeling, ain't nothing gone do no good. He's in your BLOOD. Just swimmin' 'round in dere, waiting for his chance again. Work wit 'em, dat's all Ah can tell ya. Work wit 'em and it'll be easier."

She then presented her granddaughter with the Book. Mary could hardly read English at the time, and the book was written in something she would later learn was similar to Arabic. But her grandmother helped her learn to read it in secret. From what she'd learned the Book had been written in some ancient African tribal tongue and translated by some mad Arab into the current version. This Book was one of two. The original had never been found.

She felt the leather of the Book start to pulse. It harmonized with the beating of her heart. She turned it over in her hands. Her skin and the Book's skin (for that's what the cover was, human skin) meshed together and for a moment she couldn't tell where her own hand was. She stared at the words still in the original foreign tongue. It had taken days for her little mouth to learn how to properly pronounce the title of the Book. The Demon inside whispered it through her: *NECRONOMICON.*

It had been passed down by her grandmothers over the years. From generation to generation. Brought over by a slave ship many years ago from her ancestor. She'd used the Book to free herself from bondage. At least that's what her grandmother had said.

*"She made a deal wit 'em. Like Abraham with God, she made a covenant with Arsanduolai. See, her tribe was the one dat had had the Original Book. She had it wid her at de time. She conjured him up on dat ship cause she wadn't gone be no slave, no sirree, and he came. Oh yes sir he came. Killed all dem white folks on da ship for her. Killed a lot of them slave too dough. Crashed da ship. She escaped, that's the most impordant thing. But don't nuttin' come in this world, or even the next, for free. Huh-uhh. She was a smart won dough, didn't sell **her** soul, no sir, gave him something bedder dan dat. She sold her **lineage**. Smart she was. She sold*

us. Now we pay for what she did. And ain't nuttin' you or yo pappy can do, cause you can break a deal wid da Devil, but you can't break no deal with God, no matter whose it is."

She sold her lineage. This unnamed, faceless woman had conjured an ancient deity and sold her progeny. It meant Mary's grandmother, it meant Mary, and it meant Mary's firstborn daughter. They were damned from the time they were conceived. She was nothing more than a cocoon for it. Something that was waiting to show its existence to the world again.

"Work wit 'em, and it'll be easier."

"Yeeesssssss." Mary had no idea that she was hissing in her master's voice. She didn't realize that her vision was no longer her own, nor her hearing, not even her thoughts. Even if she had she wouldn't have fought.

"Work wit 'em..."

Her sight floated upward, over the trees and weeds until she had an aerial view. Her essence wasn't in her body but in the air. She spread out over everything, saw everything at once. The white sheets, the black church, the red ground. She was omniscient. The last thing she remembered was her master, laughing. No translation needed.

◆ ❖ ◆

Arsanduolai watched from behind the trees with malevolent satisfaction as the chaos ensued. People were still on fire. The smell was overwhelming. But it was good.

"Cleanse this land! God ain't got no use for niggers!"

The leader of the KKK bellowed his commands as he got down off of his high horse. He began stalking the land, looking for any survivors. They were gonna have themselves a hanging in the name of the Lord.

His minions were fixing the rope to the tree now. A little boy, who was missing skin from most of his small body, had been found trying to crawl away. A woman who was smoldering not far away was found suitable for roping after she'd been kicked and revealed she was still alive.

They'd find more or they'd hang the bodies that were already dead just for good measure.

Whether by turning over bodies, kicking them, poking them, even shooting them he'd find someone else. This was just not enough: he wasn't satisfied. He came upon a child who had died of smoke inhalation long before. It lost its skull under his boot.

He believed they were filthy fuckers. He believed they needed to go back to Africa with their chickens, their dancing and their hollering. Now that they weren't slaves God had no use for them. No sir, His American Kingdom was for white and Christian only. Niggers need not apply.

He kicked over another body. A woman, her clothes burned into her skin. He could still make out tufts of her smoldering hair. "*Funny*," he thought, "*It still looks nappy.*" Not even fire can get the nappy out. He laughed, then wiped his boot on her best Sunday dress and made his way on.

There were still some alive to be found. Somewhere. Goddamnit he would find them too. A man, a woman, a child. Anybody. His prayers were answered when he came upon the body of a black man, his position betrayed by his coughing.

Finally…

Arsandoulai sniggered behind Mary's eyes as it watched the leader pick up the man by his collar. They listened with glee as he cursed and raved. "Ya'll niggers ain't got no business trying to start a Christian church…go back to Africa, practice ya'll's *voodoo.*"

Yep, that's *exactly* how Mary's father sounded when he said it. And now, what he had tried to become was turning on him. Jesus had sold him to the wolves.

So it was no real surprise when, upon lifting the black man up so he could be dragged to the tree, they saw that it was in fact, their father.

Vengeance is sweet.

No one saw the cloud coming.

The ten members of the Klan were too busy stringing up their victims, or desecrating bodies to see the black cloud come from atop

29

the trees. But after a moment they smelled it coming. The smell was worse than the burning flesh. It scorched its way into their lungs as it crept in behind them.

The Klan leader was the last to notice. He was in his own world, concentrating on his task. The rope was ready, and it was going to be glorious when he would smack the horse to make it leap forward to snap that nigger man's neck but good.

But he would never smack his horse.

He at last saw the plague of a cloud as it rolled over them. It reminded him of his momma's blankets, rolling on the line on Sunday morning. Wave after wave after wave.

Her blanket didn't look like this though, didn't smell like it either. His lungs just about imploded upon catching the scent. It was as if Hell had opened up and all the sulfur burned out. He would never realize the irony in his thought because it was then that all Hell did break loose.

The horses went wild. One horse jumped up so high it fell backward on its rider, who died on impact. The only exception was the horse that stood under Mary's father. It didn't move at all, as if it were obeying an unheard order to stay put.

The mighty leader of the Klan didn't know what he was going to do. He could barely breathe let alone think. He held close to the ground, trying to find fresh air. But there was only the smell of Hell, it had implanted itself into the grass and was festering in the soil.

The cloud descended and caked them with the atrocious scent and turned the night cold. It seemed like winter in a matter of seconds. He hugged his sheets to him, but that didn't make it any warmer. In fact the trademarks of the KKK became caked with ice that was so cold it became a scorching agony. Everyone began ripping off his sheets in fits of unbearable pain.

For the leader, pulling off his hood was the most painful thing he'd ever done in his life. The cloth took some skin from his neck with it as he cried in pain. His cry, however, was nothing compared with the wailing he heard coming from some unfortunate soul. He stopped struggling long enough to find out who was screaming so badly. He could have gone the rest of his life and the whole of eternity without seeing what he saw.

One of his men, he couldn't tell whom, was being attacked by what he saw as burnt black blobs. There were two of them, black as sin and checkered with small white spots. When the tears cleared from his eyes he saw that the blobs were actually two members of the congregation they'd just burned and that the checkered white spots were patches where bone jutted through. The bodies were charred so bad they were still smoking.

He spit out blood and got to his knees his mind racing with hate. What the hell was going on here? These people were supposed to be *dead*. Despite his fear he felt angry. They were *defying* him. Even in death they were defying him! His daddy had told him the only good nigger was a dead nigger and these people proved hard to put down. But their theatrics wouldn't stop him. No sir. Alive or in death they would pay dearly for their trespasses. They were acting like the savages they were. No amount of cotton was worth having them here now. Here they were killing a white man, on ground they claimed was for the Lord. They were desecrating His land with their very presence. Anger and hatred ran through his body putting his fear aside.

He began wiping the dirt and sweat from his face. The cloud had mixed with the smoke and it crusted his skin.

"Here sir, take my handkerchief."

Without thinking he snatched at the cloth and tried to wipe his face; it didn't reach, however, and as he tugged he realized it wasn't a handkerchief at all. It was the end of a dress. Through watery eyes he made out the trace of mud his boot left on her best Sunday dress.

He felt her fingernails a moment later, popping his eye clean out of its socket. He howled and dropped to his knees. There was a kick to his back, another to his ribs, chest, and multiple times to his head. He got a look at his death with one good diluted eye.

They were dead, but they were still alive. They were all alive and they were all angry.

Claws were in his skin now, as well as teeth. They were like lions with a gazelle. Pulling him apart bite by bite. He felt huge chunks of his body as they were severed. She got his other eye eventually. Only this time she stuck her claw through it to pull it out. Something pulled at his groin and after a moment, where his manhood used to be, there was nothing but a gaping, squirting fissure.

Screams filled the night air, but the cloud contained the sounds. If it hadn't been there, a person in the next county would have heard the pandemonium of slaughter. But just as quickly as it had come it soon began dying down, and he knew the End had come. He was begging God for mercy but there was none to be found. God would never look down on this area again.

Arsandoulai smiled as it used the dead congregation as puppets. It had been hundreds of years since it had animated corpses, and it had forgotten how much fun it could be. It let out another laugh, humming along to the melody of screams in the night.

Mary's father watched from his noose as the shadow of Death moved over them. It was a sight to see. The Dead had Risen. Just like the Good Book had prophesied. It wasn't the Armageddon he'd expected it to be. This wasn't peace, no lamb lying with the lion. This was only cold-blooded massacre. And somewhere in the back of his mind, he knew Mary had something to do with this. He should have let her burn to death in the Holy Water, or snapped her neck himself. Maybe she would have gone to Heaven from that, but he doubted it. She was Satan's spawn. He'd known it and he'd let her live. He could only ask God for forgiveness in his mistake as a father.

As if on cue she emerged from the forest.

Her eyes glimmered in the moonlight. As soon as she started walking, the cloud's base hovering around her head dissipated, allowing the light to show her the extent of her carnage.

"Damn you!" he shouted at her, the noose on his neck straining his words. She simply strolled toward him. Stepping over the bodies of Klan and congregation alike. It made no difference to her.

"Where was your Savior?" she asked, though it was not her voice. It was something different, something sinister. He imagined she was how the devil sounded when he tempted Jesus.

"Where was your Savior?" the Demon repeated stepping before him.

He gasped at the sight of his daughter. She was naked, and she held no shame for her condition. Her eyes were black orbs. Her skin was void of any bruises he'd inflicted earlier that evening. It was now dark and he could see her veins, as big as snakes and flowing with evil. They pulsed as she mocked him. When she spoke he saw that she had far too many teeth; it was almost impossible that she could have so many sharp objects clicking up and down. Her fingers had stretched into claws that wrapped themselves around her waist. She stood in front of him, hands on hips, as if scolding his faith. It made his heart ache to see what had come from his loins.

"As you see," the Demon said, "I give results. You don't have to wait until you die to see the fruit of your faith."

He looked upon this thing with contempt. She spoke as if she were a god.

"You beat Mary for the last time old man. I have had enough of your preaching and politics. It's time you learned. I am one of the First Named, birthed from Chaos far beyond your concept of time." Her voice made his ears bleed. He felt the liquid as it moved down his neck.

He shouted to God in Heaven for forgiveness and to damn her to Hell. His cries were interrupted by the sound of singing. He pulled his head down one last time to see,

All of his people, all of them dead stood before him some still smoldering in the night air. They were behind *her*. Behind *it*. They had all been summoned, singing "Wade in the Water." It was a sickening sound. His beliefs were being defiled, his people violated. He wanted it to end. But the horse stayed still. He realized it hadn't moved throughout the whole incident.

She had kept it there.

As the congregation joined hands and their demonic voices grew he cried for death. He cried for God to take him. His daughter stood directly beneath him, leering up at him.

"If you are so eager to go," she said, "I can send you to him."

With that she released him. A hard smack to the horse and she delivered her father to his death, his body swinging lightly in the breeze.

Arsanduolai let the bodies drop. Silence cut through the night air and a soft wind began cleaning the stench of the dead. Though it felt the

power of freedom from being called, it took one last breath of dead air and receded back into its hiding place within Mary.

Come morning local authorities would find the church in ashes and dust. The bodies were everywhere on the ground. Though seven victims would never be found, their bodies already carefully buried in a family plot. Gossip and conjecture would spread throughout the day. There had been some strange fruit hanging from the tree. Strange fruit indeed. Eight Ku Klux Klan members hung from the old oak tree with one lynched black man, who had an expression of relief on his face.

Mary wiped her calloused hands off. The family she loved had been taken care of. She wished she could be at the church to witness the discovery. But she had to leave. There would be too many unanswerable questions. Her legacy had receded back into its hiding place. Now was not the proper time to expose it. Tonight was just a demonstration. What had been broken had now been fixed. She would never again be beaten by that leather belt. This would be the last time she'd think of her father. As she looked at his body in the tree, she'd spit on him one last time and uttered to herself that Holy word, whispered it through her razor-thin smile.

"Hallelujah."

About The Author

Akela Cooper grew up loving horror movies so it's no wonder she turned into the sick and twisted individual she is today, spinning her own macabre tales when she's not working as a writer in television. Akela started her TV writing career as a staff writer on ABC's remake of the '80s lizard alien invasion miniseries *V*, moving on to NBC's fairytale cop show *Grimm* for two seasons. She currently works on the CW Network's post-apocalyptic teen drama *The 100*, as well as working her magic on Lifetime's *Witches of East End*. Akela's parents are still very, very happy they no longer have to pay her rent.

Follow her on Twitter: @akelacooper

"Three Minutes"
by Liz Edwards

T he motion sensor light turns on and shines into my room.
Someone is walking towards the house.
My pencil pauses on the second question of my take-home quiz. I wait for the sound of my mom's key in the locked door. It's only seven-twenty, too early to be back.

I run through the list of who it could be, mom—gone until at least nine, grandparents—fishing on the gulf, brother—visiting A&M, little brother—sleep over, dad—wouldn't show up without talking to mom first.

Listen.

I hear the rattle and snap as the doorknob turns and latches back into place. I wait for a response to the locked door—a key in the lock, a knock, the doorbell. My hand instinctively moves four inches to the right searching for my phone. Then I remember I don't get it back for three more days. Definitely not worth the lie about going to Megan's. Still no sound. The skin behind my ears wakes up, sensitive that something is wrong.

Get up, move. This room is a dead end. Get out.

I'm out of my chair and inching into the hallway. I hear a slow deliberate rattle, snap echo up the stairwell. The knob being tried again. No key in the lock, nothing dropped through the mail slot.

Yell. Let them know someone is home. Make it deep, masculine, like a guy.

I move to the upstairs landing ready to shout when I hear the metal squeak of the mail slot opening. Nothing falls through. They're having a look inside. Adrenaline kicks in. Pinpricks shoot down my arms, needling my skin from within.

I open my mouth but I can't control the staccato chop of quick inhales that don't reach my lungs. I'm mute, hyperventilating.

Run downstairs, go out the back, get out of the house.

I start down the stairs skipping the top step when a large, unrecognizable hand juts through the slot and searches for the knob. My eyes widen and dry out in an instant. I stumble on the top step forcing a loud creak from the wood. The sound should scare them away. The mail slot falls shut.

Run.

Left to the phone or right to the gun? Call for help. No, get the gun. Then get help. I run right to my brother's room, staying on the balls of my feet. As I reach his door, I am stopped dead by one tiny sound, a key sliding into the deadbolt.

Whoever is out there found the spare key. Anger clenches my jaw. I knew that was a stupid, obvious place to hide a key and I said nothing. She let my little brother pick it. He always gets exactly what he--

Rattle, the sound of the knob turning.

This isn't happening.

I hear the door break the threshold. I can't move.

Don't come in.

The door creaks open. A footstep on the floor. The weight of the air shifts. It's not safe here anymore. He's in my house. Standing on the glitter glue wedged between floorboards, the last mischief I shared with my little brother before we became enemies.

I hear the door close.

The knob releases in a tinny snap. In the silence the intruder is free. My mind is unable to tether him to any one physical place.

Move, move, move. Protect yourself. Get what you came for.

I close the bedroom door. Duct tape covers the absent deadlock. No way to lock it. I'm not the only one who has had things taken away. I scramble to the bed and drop to my knees. I reach. It's not there. It has to be there, he snuck it out of the safe the day after he got it.

Keep searching.

My face pushes into the comforter smelling of teenage boy and greasy fast food.

Keep stretching.

I wedge my head between the floor and metal frame. I see the outline of a case and grab it. His prized birthday present from grandpa.

Suddenly, I'm resting on my heels with it in my hand. I unzip it. I can't move fast enough. The magazine and gun slide to the carpet as I'm already searching for something to cut the cable lock. I lunge for the desk and pat the pile of debris on top. I find something solid, sharp. Scissors. I chomp the blades around the wire and saw back and forth, open and close. It's working.

The moan of weight on the wood stairs.

Load the gun, find the phone. Stay focused.

I blink away the panic. This is taking too long. I need to find the key. An image of my friend Lucia crying with laughter as we read my brother's love letters found in the false back of his bedside table. That's where he'll keep it.

I lunge for the table. My search begins and ends at the top of the table. The key is in plain sight.

I toss the scissors and grab the key. Unlike my still disabled voice, my hands are nimble, steady. I can do this. I push the key into the lock and pull the cable from the gun. I check the cartridge. It's heavy. I see two bullets inside, maybe more below.

You've watched your brother do this. Seen it in movies. It's not hard.

I push the cartridge into the handle. It slides out. I slam it into position. It clicks into place. I try not to touch the trigger as I get control of it. It's heavy.

The phone is on the other side of the stairs. I have to run past him. Too risky. I kick the case and cable lock beneath the bed, hiding evidence of the gun. Better to hide me. Where? I still need to be able to see. Indecision rises like bile.

Focus on the gun.

Where will I get the best view, be able to take the best shot. In the center of the room, facing the door. I straighten the comforter over rumpled sheets, removing any visual that shortens the mental steps to rape. I'm thankful for the extra half second my leotard and tights beneath my clothes will give me.

Don't think about that. You have a gun.

The footsteps are louder now, nearing the top of the stairs. In rapid succession, one, two. Three, four. There are two of them.

This changes nothing. Stay focused.

I back against the wall facing the door dead on. My feet are firmly on the ground. I lean against the wall for extra support but the gun pulls me to the side, stretching my arm down. My hand is getting sweaty. I almost drop it. My left hand joins my right, tight around the handle.

I look down, fully realizing that I am armed. This maims, kills.

Don't get distracted.

He probably has a gun. He does have a gun. Everyone has a gun. Holding it is not enough. I will have to use it. Make sure it's ready to fire. There are bullets in the cartridge. Get them into the chamber. I pull back the slide of the gun. It's difficult and only moves an inch. I switch hands and grip the slide with my right hand. I pull with all of my strength. An audible click. It's ready. Now what.

Maybe I should have gone for the phone. I could still hide under the bed. I won't fit.

Don't get distracted. Clear your mind.

I hear the buckle of the tops step, once, twice and then silence as feet move to the plush carpet of the landing. They are upstairs, less than eight feet from the door.

I glance at the bedside table, the twelve point buck on the cover of *Field and Stream* looks back at me, startled.

Don't get distracted. Prepare for what's coming.

I can, I will shoot. I could miss. What's the worst thing that happens. I'm shot. I die. It will be over quickly. Rape. I can take it. I can handle pain. I performed with a twisted ankle last spring. But that was an ankle, what about down there. I haven't even tried using a tampon yet. Sex is supposed to hurt, but this won't be sex. Don't fight it. It will make it worse. I can do this.

I had my period for the first time at my dad's three weeks ago. He found me on the bathroom floor rocking from side to side as my insides clenched in agony. He was smiling, proud that I had such a high pain threshold, also some crap about being a woman, but my pain threshold is what impressed him. He should know. He's a doctor. I can tolerate pain. Pain won't kill me. But he didn't have to say it in front of Mr. Neal. It was so embarrassing. God I wish my dad was here.

Focus. You are going to stop them before they do anything.

I try to hold onto the idea that I will win this. I am invincible. Even if it's not true, I need to believe it. The gun makes it true. An image from the internet last year worms its way into my head. Marcela Ruiz, a girl my age discarded in a ditch across town, stab wounds all over.

Sixty-two of them. The man who did it used zip ties to secure her then slowly sliced at her skin for an hour, cutting her all over. They found the guy, I think. They did. Yes, he's locked up. He knew the girl. I don't know anyone capable of doing that. I am a good judge of character. The darkness within someone like that would show itself. I'd see it. Wouldn't I? Sixty-two times. I sliced my finger on a can, no stiches but it hurt. A lot. Imagine that deeper … all … over.

I can't do this. I can't survive someone else doing whatever they want to me, hurting me. Not being able to stop them.

But I'm strong, I'll fight him. Does that ever work? When does the twelve year-old girl win against … anyone.

Any second now. Focus.

I have the gun. This is why it's here. Protection. I have two bullets, three, maybe more. Just aim, shoot, and keep shooting until you run out then throw it. Or hold it, have it in your hand when you jump over his body. In case he moves, you can hit him with it. Maybe I should just shoot through the door. I might miss, but maybe he'd just run away. But there are two of them if not more.

A shadow appears beneath the door.

Cold panic sets in. My mind floods with images—mom, dad, tucking me in, little brother as a baby reaching for his feet, older brother making mom cry then letting me hug him after, a blade slicing me, jabbing, stabbing, dying, dead, only a body. Please, please don't let my little brother be the one who finds me.

The knob turns.

You know what to do.

My mind clears. I am focused.

The door opens. I raise my hands, point, find the trigger.

He's big, wearing camo.

Shoot the gun. SHOOT THE GUN!

The guy behind him rushes forward. Same face as mine.

It's my brother.

The air in my throat sucks out of me. I'm instantly suffocating. I lower the gun, fumbling with it, trying to get the bullets out. I don't know how. I can't talk. I tell him with my eyes.

It's loaded, be careful.

He puts his hands around it. I won't let go. This isn't real. I'm imaging this. I'm already dead. My brother is out of town. He's not supposed to be here and then ...

The gun is out of my hands. Two quick movements and the cartridge is out, the slide disconnected. It's just metal.

It's over now.

He wraps his arms around me. My body convulses in sobs. His turn to hold me. I let him.

My eyes squeeze closed and the last few seconds play out differently. I shoot, kill them both, injure one, kill the other. It plays a dozen different ways but always ends with blood, emptiness, guilt. I cause it. Devastation, mom, dad, grandpa, little brother ...

It didn't happen. Everyone is okay. You're okay.

Relief swells and dies. Fury takes its place. Fury at the gun. Fury at where my imagination led me. Fury that I'm lucky. Fury that Marcela Ruiz wasn't. Fury that three minutes ago I was ignorant. Fury that I won't ever be again.

About The Author

Liz Edwards has spent her life telling stories, first as a choreographer in San Antonio and New York and then as a feature and documentary editor in Los Angeles (*Free a Man to Fight: Women Soldiers of World War II, Eban and Charley, The Graffiti Artist,* and numerous reality programs that shall not be named). She wrote eight episodes of *Rules of Deception* for Twentieth Television and feature thrillers for Lionsgate and High Treason. She loves to write about her worst fears naively thinking this means they won't happen to her, her husband, or her daughter.

"INT. WOLF—NIGHT"
by Jane Espenson

L ike the more common Medium-Sized Morally Neutral Wolves, Big Bad Wolves make for poor accommodations. The inside of this particular Wolf was big for an inside, but very small compared with the outside. It was about the size of a spherical single-room cottage, one with a knee-deep layer of stomach acid on the floor, but it was severely overpopulated, and there was every reason to think that more edible sentient beings might join the group at any moment. Already, Hood was assigned one-sixth of the bed and only one-tenth of the blanket. She had to fold up her red cloak to use as a pillow at night. Food, at least, was plentiful, since they ate any vegetables and non-sentient animals that the wolf ate, after the wolf ate them, so that was all right, but the toilet facilities were best left unmentioned.

Every now and then, someone, whichever of them had been there the longest, got digested. It was a revolting process in which the person/foodstuff began to lose facial definition, and it went downhill from there. The person's glasses, if he wore glasses, might suddenly slide down his nose around lunchtime, and by dinner he was a warm pool of mucus that wouldn't respond even when asked simple questions, and which ultimately seeped away into the digestive tract. The whole process looked, sounded, and smelled unpleasant, and all who lived in the Wolf knew that it was their destiny.

All in all, Hood decided, it was high time to clear out.

She kept hoping the Wolf would swallow someone in possession of a knife so that she could cut her way out, but to date that hadn't happened, and she figured she'd waited long enough. Several people in the stomach had metal on them: belt buckles, mostly. And one of the sheep had taps on his shoes, but they had no tools to pry these items loose or to sharpen them, and in their current state these items had no effect on the disgusting but resilient inside surfaces of the Wolf.

They did have two precious matches, and there had been some initial excitement over the idea of using them. "The smoke will make him sneeze us out," the littlest piggy, a babbling moron, had exclaimed, demonstrating a laughable lack of understanding of how sinuses and/or stomachs worked. Others thought they could literally burn a hole in the Wolf's side, but when they tried, the first match fizzled out against the wet stomach wall, and they were reluctant to try again and potentially waste the one remaining match. Besides, several sheep, whose luxuriant curls were rich and oily with lanolin, had raised monotonous issues about their flammability that had exhausted everyone else. Finally, the remaining match was wrapped in oilskin and tucked into Hood's belt to be used when anyone could think of a sensible plan.

The Boy Who Cried Wolf had tried an escape a few days back, making the daring move of plunging deeper into the Wolf's digestive system. He had returned filthy and gasping, his eyes streaming, and trembling all over. He wove a harrowing tale of darkness, confining walls, and choking gases. He, however, was a famous alarmist, so it was possible that he was exaggerating.

Hood considered the other direction: the mouth. From the throat, by peeking up from under the Wolf's pink, globe-sized and frankly disturbing uvula, she could survey the area. The teeth, clearly, were the primary problem. Ten inches long, and as razor-sharp on all their edges as if they'd been honed on a strop, they rimmed the mouth like white steel blades, some bristling at odd angles, designed to snag and catch. Hood leaned her back against the hot plane of the Wolf's throat, out of the dank draft of wolf breath, and tried to think. She kept thinking she should have reacted better when faced with a Wolf in her grandmother's bed.

"Oh, Grandma, what big eyes you have!" She'd meant it only as a delaying tactic, of course. Hood's grandmother was a tiny woman, ninety pounds at most, and to the best of Hood's recollection, she was almost entirely not covered by a shaggy, musty pelt. The massive creature tucked under the sheets of her grandmother's bed managed to look both absurd and terrifying, with the tiny white linen bedcap clinging to one rough ear, and the tail end of Granny's pajama-pants drawstring dangling damply from its powerful jaw. While the muscle-bound creature struggled to find a witty retort to the "big eye" observation, Hood was backing toward the door, readying her basket in front of her as a shield. When the Wolf had opened his mouth to reply, she could hear the shouts of the helpless creatures inside. "Hey!" "Is someone out there?" "Little help?" and beyond, the frantic tip-tip-tipping sound of the sheep wearing tap shoes.

She reached behind her, groping for the doorknob. But the Wolf, despite its size, was lightning fast. He covered the length of the cabin in one stride. Hood had been aware of heat, darkness, the brush-and-catch of those fearsome teeth, and then being forced down the wet throat by a series of muscular contractions like a horrible stinking reverse birth. Finally, she landed on the stomach floor with a splash, her basket landing behind her with a smaller, cuter splash. She sat up and looked around, stunned, at the dull-eyed residents, who immediately started cordoning off a small section of the bed for her, and grudgingly shifted their own belongings from one locker into another to make room.

But as she gathered herself, and wrung out her cape, Hood took heart. Because her grandmother wasn't there. Over the days that followed, she asked around. It was Bo Peep who was most willing to talk. An old lady had been here recently, she confided, arriving perhaps a week ago. On the fourth morning after her arrival, they'd awoken to discover she was missing. Some of them, primarily the cows, felt that she'd been a victim of Sudden Spontaneous Digestion and had seeped away unnoticed, but Hood knew better. Granny had escaped. And that meant there was a way out. "If she can do it, I can do it," Hood vowed.

But, oh, those teeth. The Wolf had an irresponsible tendency to gulp without chewing on the way in, but Hood had a feeling that the way out would be different. She crawled higher in the mouth, the tongue sinking under her feet like a carpet made out of slugs, as she angled for a closer look. She heard a faint whiny bleating. She looked around and spotted a very small lamb waving a hoof. Its fleece was white as snow, and a diamond tennis bracelet glinted at her from its slender wrist. The lamb blinked hopefully from where it was caught, unhurt, between two molars, a forgotten morsel. The lamb explained, a little haughtily, that it was stuck, as it continued to offer her its tiny entitled hoof. Hood pulled it out and tucked it under her arm, where it immediately fell into a petulant sleep; then she turned her back on the frightening red cavern. The mouth, that stinking red room rimmed with death, was a way out. It may even have been her grandmother's way out. But Hood was no fool. Those teeth terrified her. This wasn't her way out.

Back in the stomach, she reunited the sleeping and flatulent lamb with its ungrateful family. Then she waited for nightfall, when it would be time to head for the other way out. She hoped to be forcing her head out into clear night air before anyone even noticed she was missing. And yet, despite her hope, she checked her belt, to make sure the small oilskin packet was still there. "You never know," she thought, which was an excellent mantra for someone who lived in a stomach.

The difference in the amount of light available inside a wolf during daylight and at night is negligible, but noticeable, and it wasn't long before all the inhabitants of the Wolf were sound asleep, except for the duck, the other duck, and the goose who had formed a doo-wop trio that practiced until all hours—and Hood. She slipped out of bed, grabbed her cloak, and headed down deeper into the Wolf.

The Boy had been right, of course, and the passage was slick and foul and choked with gas. But Hood pressed on, determined. She wondered as she went, as she had wondered many times before, where Granny might have gone after escaping. Hood was sure she hadn't been in the cabin, and if she'd been nearby, she surely would have flagged down Hood and warned her away. Most likely, she'd gone for help, but it could take her weeks to return with assistance, and even then, there was no reason to assume that any would-be rescuer wouldn't just join the rest of them inside the Wolf interior space. Hood was confident she was doing the right thing. If only she could breathe.

That was, in fact, becoming a daunting challenge. Her vision was cloudy, and thinking was becoming difficult. Hood thought about turning back, but she'd moved quickly, hurrying to get far enough that turning back would be impossible. She didn't want to give herself an easy way out.

Finally, her knees buckled and she sank to the slimy floor. She fumbled, clumsy and half-blind, for the oilskin packet under her belt.

It had been a fine life, she thought. She'd dined with bears. She'd pulled thorns from the paws of echidnas. She'd wrestled giant snails for money. She, at least until now, had lived.

She pulled her red cloak tight around her, making sure to cover her head and hands. The cloak was old and worn; Granny had woven it for her years ago out of thick plastic sheeting and long strips of steel wool sprayed with a red rust-proofing solution. It was meant to protect her from whale attacks, not this, but it would have to do.

She pulled the cloak tighter and struck the match.

Later on, Hood faced other challenges in her life. When she was thirty, she would slay a dragon and rescue a prince from a tower. When she was fifty, she and her daughter would surf the great salt sea on a board made of a paralyzed badger. When she was eighty, she would hand-raise a baby Big Bad Wolf, and show it another way to live. Exploding a wolf to death from the inside wasn't even something she was particularly proud of; maybe there was a better solution. But in the moment, it was what she chose.

She would always remember that the methane explosion was muffled, more WOOMPH than BANG. And it was with a surprisingly gentle and graceful motion that the now-headless Wolf's skin folded down in panels and opened like the blooming of a flower, revealing the trapped beings and their furnishings inside, startled and blinking at the light and half-deafened by the explosion. A single pure-white lamb was the first to stagger free, already complaining.

Hood was the most severely injured, her hands burned and her lungs aching. The cloak had protected her to the best of its ability, though, and she was safe.

She was burned, but she was strong. She had found her own path, but it was inspired by someone who had gone before. She had made a hard choice, but she was willing to live with the consequences.

Soon, her grandmother arrived with help at the site of the explosion. Hood held her grandmother's hand and listened to the professional chatter of all the king's horses and all the king's men as they tended to the injured. Hood lay on her back and looked up at the sky and smiled. Tomorrow would be a better day.

About The Author

Jane Espenson is known for her work as a writer for *Dinosaurs*, *Ellen*, *Buffy the Vampire Slayer*, *Angel*, *Firefly*, *Dollhouse*, *The O.C.*, *Gilmore Girls*, *Tru Calling*, *Battlestar Galactica*, *Caprica*, and *Game of Thrones* among other shows. She is co-creator of the award-winning online comedy *Husbands* along with her producing partner Brad Bell (@GoCheeksGo). She also writes comic books, short stories, and edits collections of essays. She currently writes for ABC's *Once Upon A Time*.

Follow her on Twitter: @JaneEspenson
Watch "Husbands" online: www.husbandstheseries.com

"XAYMACA"
by Shalisha Francis & Nadine Knight

"Y*ou spit inna the sky, it fall inna yuh eye.*"
How many times had Sisu heard that phrase as a girl? Reaping what you'd sown: a favorite adage told in a family of farmers. She'd hear it from her dad in chastising tones if she procrastinated on studying for her A-levels. From her Auntie Shirley if she yanked her cousin's head while locking his hair. And if she set off down the mountain late—missing the chance to hawk their family's produce to the tourists who overwhelmed the Port Royal marina—her Mama would practically shout the words at her.

"*You spit inna the sky, it fall inna yuh eye.*"

But Sisu would just roll her eyes and laugh. At them, at the island sayings, at herself. Sisu used to laugh a lot. Things aren't so funny anymore.

Because someone did spit in the sky. Well, some *fool* country did anyhow. Sent up rovers into space searching for E.T. or God or some other stupidness. The Investors, or so they named themselves, followed one of the rovers back to Earth. Set up shop. She'd been in Kingston when she'd first heard the news. Had taken two bus transfers and walked a half mile in the sticky heat to reach the heart of town. Still, she'd been happy to go. Happy for the small taste of freedom the trip afforded her—a day free of shucking sugar cane, climbing coconut trees, or haggling with foreigners. She'd been carrying her bag of purchases—sweeties for her cousin, good American shampoo, a beef patty—and was set to make the long journey home when she saw the crowd outside the pawnshop. They were clustered around the second-hand flat screens in the display window.

It wasn't the crowd itself that caught her attention—it wasn't rare to see Jamaicans gathered around a TV to cheer their favorite team in a cricket match or crow with pride over Usain Bolt's latest world record—here, it was their faces. A mix of natives and foreigners, each expression more distressed than the last. Curious, she'd crowded in behind them, followed their gazes to the scratchy fifty-two inch screens. Watched as Investor ships appeared in the skies over all the major cities in the world—well, the "first world," anyway. As the stunned crowd huddled together, Sisu remembers feeling cold for the first time, the kind of bone-deep chill life in the Caribbean had always spared her. She remembers noticing the foreigners no longer clutched their money holders under their shirts. As if they knew money would no longer give them power or comfort, that the world had been instantly and irrevocably changed.

The Investors announced they were there to help the world "reach its full potential" and "run more efficiently." But though they spoke in the local languages of every land they occupied, no one knew, no one yet understood, what they meant by that. What they did know was the Investors were impervious to most of the world's weaponry. They'd figured that out soon enough. From what Sisu had gleaned from the occasional television feeds and radio broadcasts that still made it through, North Korea tried sending a nuke, but only ended up obliterating its own people; only slowed the Investors down for half a day. Sisu also knows that, contrary to the matinees she'd seen at the local dollar theater, alien invasion has not united the world: Russia and the States were threatening each other, China had threatened Japan and South Korea, and much of the EU was in chaos as they tried to agree on a response. She and her countrymen had watched and fretted, expecting to soon see the giant metal ships over their skies. But days passed, then weeks, and still the only Investors they saw were on TV.

At first glance, their unsettling appearance—the pale, almost translucent, skin; the iridescence of their humanoid form—seemed a product of poor television reception. But Sisu soon learned, through eyewitness accounts she'd found on the now defunct Internet, that her first impression had been accurate. To her, they looked like how she'd always imagined *obeah men* would. As a girl, she'd been terrified *obeah men* were hiding in the shadows or under her bed, waiting to put a curse on her or steal her away. Now, at nineteen, it's the pale face of the

Investors that keeps her awake in the night, that keeps her in a constant state of worry. Her Auntie Shirley swears their island's been spared. That she and her old biddies at the Kingston Baptist church managed to pray the Investors away. Why else had they not come?

"Cause we nuh matter," Sisu's Mama would hiss in return, *"What sense it mek to take care of de ants in de yahd before yuh tend de rats in de kitchen?"*

So for once, Sisu was glad to have little money and to be from a land that was considered thoroughly unworthy of notice. And she and her fellow islanders can only hope it stays that way. At least until they understand what this not-so-brave new world will become. They already knew their new world was dangerous. *Her parents*—No. Sisu shakes the thought from her head. Not now. Now, she must focus on the task at hand.

She loads up her rickety cart with bananas, ackee, and breadfruit. With coffee from further up this south side of the Blue Mountains, already hastily ground and dumped in a few burlap sacks. Its aroma clashes with the heaping baskets of mangoes she heaves on top. As she adds to the pile, she gives her skin-and-bone horse, Winston, an apologetic pat. Time was, they'd drive him in a truck closer to Port Royal. But her truck and trailer were long gone. Now Winston was being asked to do long journeys on little food and it had taken its toll. Sisu is already steeling herself for his loss, too.

As she sets off down the mountain, she smiles at the cart her Mama had bought thinking it would attract tourists to their stand in the marina. Sisu had always felt they romanticized the past too much for ignorant tourists who wanted things quaint and exotic, but she was grateful for the cart now, grateful to have transport now that there was no fuel on the island.

Good thing she knows the route well, that she's used to carting food down the mountain. Now, though, she brings it to the newly-named United Defense Forces. A grand name for what is mostly a bizarre alliance between the police and the better-armed gangs from Kingston, finding, for once, common interest in shooting at the mainlanders who try to find refuge on their island. It began with cruise ships and tourists who outstayed their normal single-day welcome, who couldn't leave the island after the Investors suspended air travel or who feared what they might find at home upon their return. But the island could not support these extra people. Especially not when they, in all their entitled arrogance, demanded to take over, to tell their Prime Minister what to do. PM Morgan had, for once, had the country's entire agreement when she decided to ignore the calls upon Commonwealth loyalty and concede their land as a satellite base. That would just bring the trouble here even faster. And the ants need to stay beneath notice for as long as they can.

That's not to say that things are entirely safe here. The chaos had hit Jamaica, too: opportunists and thieves and fanatics who used the invasion as an excuse for their own wicked desires. *Her parents*—no, no thinking about that, not when she needs her eyes free of tears to make out the hazards of the road by moonlight. So, even when she passes what's left of her home she doesn't look. Refuses to acknowledge the two recent graves, some bits of greenery beginning to emerge from the dirt.

Sisu must keep moving. She's running late—again. She tells herself that waiting for the full moon to rise will make this nighttime trip less treacherous, though she has been making the trip for years. Traveling through the night used to give her the chance to meet the sunrise at the waterline, set up her wares for sale. Nowadays, she hopes it will keep her safer, keep her out of anyone's notice, while it seems like the whole island is armed and wary and waiting to see what will happen to them next. It's like waiting for a hurricane to come, only worse. There doesn't seem to be any hope this will pass quickly or blow itself away. Sisu's accepted that there probably won't be an end to this. Six weeks in and she's becoming, at last, practical. A Powell. The Powell family had always been very practical, had made their living off the land and the tanned, eager tourists for generations now.

Nuh Powells nuh quit.

It's become her mantra. The thing that reminds her she's a farmer, the daughter and great granddaughter of farmers and, before them, slaves brought against their will to work this beautiful, mountainous island. She will not disrespect her ancestors by lying down now, not when slavery and rebellion and liberty are in her blood. She survives as her ancestors have, by retreating up the mountains and into the shadowy gullies. Retreat is, after all, an effective means of resistance. It had served her well after their farm was attacked, after looters snuck onto their land in the dead of night, raided every inch for livestock, fruits, and vegetables. When her dad ordered her to run, Sisu took off up the road—her feet bare, her hair still tightly wrapped in her head scarf. She'd hid in a small cave she'd played in as a child, trembling in a corner. It was a full twenty minutes before she realized the bandits weren't coming after her, a full three days before she understood her parents weren't either. So the cave has become her new home. It provides her good cover, and there is even a grassy corner where she is beginning a new garden.

As she arrives at the first checkpoint, the guard recognizes Winston and her wobbly cart, waves her through. She moves past the skittery hairpin curve that always makes her queasy and happy she can't actually see the drop off, and past Eleven Mile village, popular in legend as the home of a rebellious slave. These legends are found all over the island, and Sisu hopes their ghosts are keeping watch over them now. The highway smooths out as much as it ever does, and it's just another 20 kilometers or so to her final destination. Time will be tight with Winston's slow, footsore pace.

Today she's stopped at the second checkpoint. The flirty UDF guard on the right throws her a whistle and a wink before relieving her of her supplies. Saves her the trip all the way to the end of the spit, then. Good. He doesn't give her cash. What's the point of money right now? Some *fool-fools* had taken money, as if a mix of Jamaican dollars and a few scattered Euros would be accepted anywhere. No, Sisu has taken easily to the barter system and is smart enough to ask for batteries, scrap metal, and kerosene instead. When even that becomes too rare, she will ask for any spare tires or cured ironwood they had left over—the pieces too small for use on the blockade, but good enough to shore up her cart and her vegetable beds.

Almost sunrise now, the sky lighting to cobalt and a hint of orange. Sisu carefully reins Winston to an old pull-off from the highway, finds the narrow stone path down to a small cove. Tourists used to love it here, thinking they'd found a secret lover's beach. Locals would sometimes fleece their cars for any valuables left behind, or wait impatiently for their return to sell them fresh squeezed cane juice or coconuts they hacked with a machete to open for drinking. No one is on the beaches much these days. Right now the UDF is focused on keeping people from coming to shore, not on anyone heading towards the water. No one will notice her here, and the sweeping watchlights are being powered down to spare them this close to daylight. Giant signs offshore proclaim FOREIGN GO HOME!, as does the occasional blaring loudspeaker if an unknown vessel comes into sight. The UDF had chased off a few giant cruise ships early on, but things had been quiet for the last fortnight. The friendlier of the two men at the first checkpoint told her, on her last trip down, that the Prime Minister was worried that more were amassing. Assuming the Investors hadn't already taken care of them, that is.

But just today, just for a few minutes, Sisu wants to pretend everything's *irie*, like the last several weeks haven't happened. She wants to stick her toes in the surf and greet the morning. Maybe even catch a small snapper or two for supper. She toes off her sandals and heaves a shaky breath. She can do this. She can keep surviving. She dips her feet in the warm water. Pretends the sand beneath her toes is a spa treatment like the ones you get at the *stush* all-inclusive resorts. And so, her next breath is easier and the one after that freer still. The weather will be good today, she can tell by the lack of pain in her ankle and by clear skies turning bright on the horizon. Sisu looks down at her wiggling toes and fumbles in the pocket of her trousers for a hook and some line.

She hears some muffled splashing first. Sound carries far over water. She ignores it, assumes it's a local fisherman out or someone like herself. But then, she hears more.

"*No—this way!*" in a woman's voice and "*Quiet!*" in a different register. And neither voice was Jamaican.

"*What—what de hell?*" she breathed.

Heart suddenly pounding, Sisu stared as hard as she could out to sea. Surely she was imagining things. But—was that really a raft? How did it get here? And how come the UDF didn't spot it? She should probably raise the alarm. It's what they've been told to do. And one strong shout would bring at least a dozen UDF to the clearing. But for the folks on that raft her call would mean certain death. And though it had only been six weeks since the Investors threw the world into chaos, Sisu is already tired of death.

So she runs down the beach, rushes up to the two men and woman dragging their raft onto shore.

"You must hide it," she whispers urgently.

Three pairs of eyes turn towards her, guarded, defensive. She stops. Holds up her hands in peace.

"Your raft. You must hide it. The next shift's goin' pass by in a few." They didn't want to alert the UDF to their trespassing, did they? And though the refugees could certainly hide amongst the thick trees surrounding the cove, the raft would give them away. Did they want to spend the next few hours running from trigger-happy UDF guards?

Sisu hears their sighs of relief, sees their shoulders relax as they realize she won't betray them. One of the men, the younger of the two, steps forward, tells her his name's Aidan. The other two, an older man with grey tinged hair and a willowy redheaded girl, attempt to carry their cargo off the raft. Wait, not cargo—a young boy, maybe seventeen. But he's not moving. The girl begins to shake him, the color draining from her sunburned face, her whispers turning to cries. Sisu watches in pity as realization and grief hit the girl, knows when her mouth falls open she's primed to wail, to give away their location and bring the UDF running. Alarmed, Sisu moves to hush her, but the older man is quicker. His hand clamps over her mouth, muting her screams. He's sorry, very sorry, but there's nothing to be done for her friend. He holds her as her body trembles, as it shakes open his coat, revealing a small vial hanging from his necklace. It's too dark to see what's inside, but when he catches Sisu looking at it, he tucks it under his shirt.

Aidan calls her attention to the horizon, his brow furrowed with worry. The sun will be up soon. They can't stay here much longer. He wants to know if Sisu can help them, hide them. And for some reason she does not know, Sisu says yes, shakes off the guilt of betraying her countrymen, her homeland. A few stowaways aren't going to sink the island.

They hide the body and raft under sand and palm tree branches, head back to where Winston waits patiently with the cart. After she helps the three climb inside, she uses her newly gotten scrap metal to cover them, throws some rotten fruit on top to discourage checkpoint guards from looking too closely. She only hopes Winston, his body shaking and straining from the extra weight, won't give them away.

This time, when the checkpoint guard favors her with a wink and smile, she flirts back. Hopes it seems natural, hopes he won't notice her shaking hands. Luckily, he waves her through. Just in time, too, because soon after, Winston falters, stumbles. His meager body trembling under the strain, he refuses to move any further up the mountain. Sisu guides him off the road, unhitches him, gives his rump a firm pat—he'll have to find his own way. They must find theirs. The sun will be up soon and they must hurry.

As she leads her companions into the canyon stretching down below, Aidan seems familiar with it, guesses they're in a gully near Judgment Cliff.

"You've come this way before?" Sisu asks, surprised.

After slight hesitation, he says no, he's only heard of it. But the path wasn't usually mentioned to tourists for fear they'd attempt it. With scratchy, thick foliage and steep, rocky inclines made slippery by resilient moss, the terrain was far too rough.

Still, the two men take the climb in stride, even the older one, which given his gold watch and manicured hands surprises Sisu. But the woman, who Aidan says is called Lena, frets the whole way. Do they even know where they're going? What if they die out here in the middle of nowhere? Her mumblings are in English, but with a hint of something else—French, maybe—and Sisu pays more attention to her accent than her words. But Lena's male companions try desperately to shush her, seem worried Sisu will take offense. As if they believe she will tire of Lena and abandon them to navigate the treacherous terrain on their own. But Sisu's dealt with people like Lena before. Foreigners, scared and out of their element, a long way from the familiar, from the soothing comfort of home. So she takes her hand, gives it a firm squeeze, tells Lena the same thing she used to tell them.

"Everyt'ing goin' be alright."

She's not sure Lena believes her, not sure she can believe it herself. But as she leads the three strangers back to her home, she tries to draw hope from her family's favored saying. Tries to believe that somehow, saving these three might reap unforeseen fortune or garner her some goodwill. That perhaps, this one generous act will be the key to her survival.

About The Authors

Shalisha Francis has been obsessed with the art of storytelling since she was a little girl begging for one more story before bed time. This fixation persisted through her study of Comparative Literature at Princeton and even through her years practicing law at Proskauer Rose and Warner Bros. Records. Thankfully, her current career as a television writer allows her not only to read intriguing stories, but to create them as well. Her writing credits include *Castle* and *Marvel's Agents of S.H.I.E.L.D.*

Nadine M. Knight is an Assistant Professor of English at College of the Holy Cross in Worcester, MA. Her teaching and research interests include African American literature, Civil War narratives, and film and television studies. She usually divides her time between paging through 150 year-old diaries in special manuscript collections and watching shows like *The Wire* or *The Bridge* for academic articles, and she welcomes any Civil War diaries or television recommendations you can offer.

"Collapse"
by Lisa Klink

We were out on a call when the earth started to shake. It was the third time in two months that our ambulance crew had been dispatched to this particular address, home of 77-year-old Edgar Sullivan. He had called 911 complaining of chest pains. Again.

Mr. Sullivan was one of our "frequent fliers," who summoned emergency services every so often just to break up the monotony of his solitary, post-retirement life. We'd known this was a false alarm even before we left the station, but we couldn't exactly ignore the call. So here we were, in a small, overstuffed apartment on a miserably hot day, dutifully listening to Mr. Sullivan's heart and assuring him that he was not having a heart attack. Again.

"If you're really concerned," Davis told him, "we could take you to the hospital for some tests."

The old man waved his hand, dismissing the suggestion. This was all part of the usual script. To Davis's credit, he didn't sound nearly as exasperated as I would have. He had a calm, confident manner that patients with real emergencies found comforting. I was crabby from a stupid fight I'd had with Jeff this morning about buying a new car, which had turned into another round of prudent husband/irresponsible wife.

I was jolted back to reality by a violent tremor that knocked me off my feet. Books rained down from the overstuffed shelves. One clocked me on the forehead before I remembered to duck and cover. A lamp slid off the end table and smashed next to me. Kitchen cabinets flew open, and a cascade of dishes poured out, breaking on the tile floor.

Outside, a dozen car alarms blared to life. We heard a mighty crash of concrete and glass.

Then it was over. I looked up to see that Davis had pulled Mr. Sullivan under the dining table, like you're supposed to do in an earthquake. They were both unhurt. A rivulet of blood ran down my forehead, and I swiped it away, wincing as I touched the rapidly swelling spot where the book had hit.

The apartment looked like a tornado had come through. The living room was littered with books and knickknacks, and the narrow kitchenette was at least a foot deep in broken glasses, bowls, and plates. I glanced at the LED display on the microwave and saw it was dark. The power was out.

The three of us headed outside. The temperature had risen by at least ten degrees while we were in Mr. Sullivan's apartment. Our ambulance driver, Alex, was on his way in to find us. "Are you guys all right?" he asked.

We confirmed that everyone was fine. Then we saw how lucky we'd been. Across the street, a four-story apartment building had collapsed into a huge pile of rubble. The building had an open first floor for parking, and the concrete pillars that supported the whole structure had crumbled. The floors above had pancaked, landing on top of one another in a mess of bricks, drywall, and crushed furniture. It was almost noon on a Tuesday, so most of the residents should be at work or school. Most of them.

Alex went back to the ambulance to call Fire Station 72, our home base. Neighbors were starting to emerge from the other, undamaged buildings on the street. Some of them were hurt, mostly cuts and bruises. A tall man with a scruffy goatee was cradling his wrist. For a moment, he reminded me of Jeff.

Jeff. I hadn't even thought about him. I was a terrible wife. I pulled out my cell phone to call him. No service. Of course. Phone lines and cell towers were probably down all over the city. But we had an emergency plan. Jeff kept a radio in his desk. He would use it to contact Fire Station 72, which would relay a message to me. That was assuming Jeff could reach his desk. In the really tall building where he worked. He was fine, I told myself. Perfectly fine. Those angry words this morning wouldn't...couldn't...be our last.

I shoved those thoughts away. I had a job to do. People on the street had seen the ambulance and were heading our way, seeking medical attention and information about the quake. How strong was it? Was there a lot of damage? Why wouldn't their phones work? We had precious little information to give, only what Alex could gather on the radio. The quake was estimated at 6.5 on the Richter scale, and the epicenter was somewhere east of downtown. That was it. No word on emergency response. No message for me.

I was removing a shard of glass from a girl's arm when a stocky, middle-aged woman pushed her way through the waiting patients. "You have to help me!" she insisted. "He's trapped!"

"Who's trapped?" I asked.

"My brother. He lives in that building," she said urgently.

I finished extracting the glass and taped a square of gauze over the wound. Then I turned to the woman. Her name, I learned later, was Bianca. "Where is he?"

She took my arm and pulled me to a section of the collapsed building, where there was a gap between chunks of concrete. She leaned in and shouted, "Manuel!"

A faint voice issued from the opening. "Get me out!"

"I'm a paramedic," I called to the man. "Can you move?"

"My legs are trapped!" he yelled back. "Help me!"

"We will," I promised, not quite sure how. Manuel was buried under a two story mountain of debris that would take some serious equipment to remove.

I went to Alex. "How soon can we get a heavy rescue crew?"

He relayed this request to the dispatcher, who informed us that calls were coming in from all over the city and every crew was already occupied. She would put us on the waiting list, and, no, she couldn't tell us how long the wait would be. Translation: very long.

"So what are we supposed to do in the meanwhile?" I demanded of Alex and Davis. "Just leave him there?"

"Nothing else we can do," said Davis, in that calm, reasonable tone that patients always found so comforting. I didn't.

I returned to the pile of debris. Bianca looked up at me hopefully. I knelt beside her and shouted into the opening, "Manuel. Can you tell me about your injuries?"

"I know my legs are hurt, but I can't see them. They're under a lot of bricks," he told me.

I tried to imagine the scene. "Can you move the bricks? Enough to pull your legs out?"

He let out a short, pained laugh. "I can't even reach them. I'm on my stomach and I can't fucking move!"

I considered the gap between the concrete chunks. It was big enough for a person to fit through. I pulled out my mini-flashlight and shone it through the opening. A rough passageway extended at least ten feet into the rubble. A splintered piece of plywood obscured the rest.

"I see light!" shouted Manuel. The flashlight beam was shining through the cracks in the plywood, all the way to Manuel. There had to be at least a small, clear path. I should be able to reach him. Last year, I had taken a month of urban search and rescue training. I just needed to remember what the hell I'd learned.

The earth trembled again. The aftershock wasn't as strong as the initial jolt, but just as frightening. A few people screamed. Some dropped into a protective huddle, arms shielding their heads. The big pile of rubble shifted and settled. From within it, Manuel cried out in pain.

I shouted into the opening. "Manuel? Are you all right?"

"No!" he yelled. "I'm under a fucking building."

I went to my colleagues. "We have to get him out. I think I can reach him."

Davis disagreed. "It's too dangerous. We need to wait for heavy rescue."

"Do you know how long that could take?" I demanded. "He probably has crush injuries to both legs. He needs treatment. Now."

He was unmoved. "I'm sorry. We wait."

I looked to Alex, who wanted no part of this debate. "We wait," he echoed.

I paced. Technically, Davis is the senior guy on our crew. But that doesn't make him my boss. Technically. So I simply said, "No."

I climbed into the back of the ambulance and started looking for supplies. We had to have tools in here somewhere.

"Erin..." Davis began, coming up beside me.

"We can't wait. That whole thing is going to collapse on him," I argued.

"And you, if you go in there," he pointed out.

I opened a wall cabinet and found only bandages and gauze. "It's dangerous. I accept that. You want me to sign a waiver or something?"

"I want to save the guy, too. Sometimes, we just can't." He caught my arm and made me look at him. "You know that."

I did. This was a stupid risk. But I couldn't walk away. When I talked with the man under the building, I didn't hear Manuel. I heard Jeff, trapped alone somewhere, waiting for a rescue that didn't come. I knew perfectly well how unlikely that was. He was probably fine. Even if he wasn't, I couldn't help him by risking my life to rescue a stranger. But, as crazy as it was, giving up on one man felt like giving up on both. I wasn't ready to do that.

"You know what I could really use? A crowbar." I pulled away from Davis and opened a hatch in the floor. Bingo. A spare tire and everything you need to change it out. The car jack was too bulky to carry with me, but the jack handle would work as a substitute crowbar. I took it.

I checked in with Alex one more time, in the faint hope that he would tell me a heavy rescue crew was already on its way. Or, maybe, that my husband was alive. Nothing.

I went back to the pile of debris. Bianca was sitting by the opening, talking to Manuel, reassuring him that he'd be saved. I crouched beside her and called to him. "Manuel, I'm coming."

"Wait." It was Davis, striding toward me with a long coil of nylon rope. I didn't think he would actually tie me up to stop me. Would he? He handed me one end of the rope. "At least put on a safety line."

"Right." I took the rope and threaded it through my belt loops. My search and rescue instructors had insisted on safety lines for every exercise. They had also insisted on safety helmets. We didn't carry helmets in the ambulance. We weren't supposed to do anything that required them.

I tied the rope at my waist and turned to Davis. "Thanks."

There was nothing left to do but do it. I slid the metal jack handle down the back of my shirt, leaving my hands free as I climbed into the small opening. I crawled forward over uneven debris, choosing the most stable-looking spots to put my weight. There was a large slab of concrete overhead, forming the roof of this little tunnel. I tried not to think of the mountain of rubble on top of that. Which was like trying not to think of an elephant. You can't help it.

Sunlight shone in from behind me, growing fainter as I went further in. I pulled the mini-flashlight from my pocket and held it in my mouth as I pushed forward. It was even hotter in here than it had been outside. I was sweating heavily. I had to stop every so often to wipe my forehead against the sleeve of my T-shirt.

Then I put my hand on an unstable pile of rocks, which collapsed under my weight. I slipped, smacking my chin against a piece of steel rebar. My teeth chomped down on the little flashlight and I let out a squawk of pain.

"Erin? You okay?" Davis asked immediately.

I spit out the flashlight, along with a bloody chunk of tooth, and answered, "I'm fine." Davis was right. This was insane. The smart thing to do was turn around and get out. Sure, I could do that. Manuel couldn't.

It occurred to me to check on him. "Manuel?" I shouted.

"Yeah?" he answered. His voice sounded tired. It also sounded close.

"Hang on, all right? I'm almost there." He didn't respond. I put the mini-flashlight between my left thumb and forefinger and continued to crawl. The final stretch was really tight. I had to turn on my side and use my legs to push myself a couple of inches at a time. If this guy was pudgy, we were in trouble.

I emerged into a somewhat larger space, maybe the size of a small bathroom. It felt huge. The ceiling of this room had mostly collapsed, but Manuel had been lucky. The exterior walls of the building were made of solid brick. He was in an end unit where two of those walls met. That corner had been strong enough to stay standing during the earthquake, and hold up part of the ceiling as it fell in, creating this cozy, survivable void.

But another section of the brick wall had failed. It had toppled into Manuel's apartment, crushing his legs. I found him lying on his stomach, the lower part of his body buried under a pile of bricks. His size wouldn't be an issue. The man was positively scrawny.

He looked up at me, his face taut with pain. I took his hand. "I'm Erin. I'm going to get you out of here."

66

Manuel squeezed my hand. "Thank you."

I glanced over the visible part of his body but saw no major damage. Then I turned to the rubble covering his legs. I pulled away some loose bricks, but the real problem was a solid piece of wall, about two feet tall and three feet wide. It wasn't huge, but very heavy. Which is why I had brought my improvised crowbar. I pulled it from the back of my shirt.

The next aftershock was a strong one. As the mountain of debris rumbled ominously around us, I threw my body over Manuel's. A chunk of plaster hit my back, doing no real damage. A larger piece of concrete landed inches from my head.

"It's all right, we're all right," I said, reassuring both my patient and myself. Manuel's lips moved in rapid, silent prayer.

Then everything went still. I straightened up, feeling the bruise on my back, but nothing worse. "Are you okay?" I asked Manuel. "Relatively speaking."

He nodded, but his movements were slow and his eyes looked bleary. He was fading.

Davis shouted from outside. "Erin?"

I called back, "We're okay." *For now,* I couldn't help thinking. We had to get moving.

I looked around for something I could use as a fulcrum. There was a wealth of choices in the debris. I picked up a piece of concrete and placed it near the brick wall.

"I'm going to lift that chunk of wall, and you're going to pull your legs out," I told Manuel.

He looked dubious. "Lift it?"

I held up the jack handle. "With this." I wedged one end under the brick wall and leaned it against the fulcrum. "Give me a lever and I can move the world, right?"

That won me a faint smile. "On the count of three, I lift and you pull," I said. He nodded. "Are you ready?" Another nod. "One...two...three!"

On the last word, I pushed down on the handle with all the force I could muster, throwing my whole weight on it. The wall lifted a couple of inches, then a little more. It was all I could do.

It was enough. Manuel reached down and hauled his damaged legs out of harm's way, crying out in pain as he did. When he was clear, I let go of the handle and the heavy wall crashed again.

"Still okay," I called to Davis, anticipating his reaction to the sound.

I turned back to Manuel, and for a horrible moment, I thought he was dead. I quickly touched his neck and felt a pulse. I could see him breathing. He had passed out from the effort and pain. I couldn't blame him.

Manuel's jeans were torn and soaked with blood. His left leg seemed to have gotten the worst of it. A broken bone jutted from an open wound below the knee, and his foot dangled loosely from the ankle. To have any chance of saving the leg, he needed a hospital. Now.

First, I had to get him out of this concrete tomb. Could I back my way through the narrow tunnel and drag him along with me? Even if I could manage it, which I doubted, it would be excruciatingly slow. Then I remembered I had a lifeline. A literal line of rope connecting me to safety. I untied the nylon rope from my waist. Then I looped it around Manuel's chest, under the armpits, and secured it with an extra knot, just to be safe.

I shouted to Davis. "He's unconscious. I need you to pull him out."

A moment as he considered this. "Okay. We can use the…"

"Safety line," I concluded. "Already tied and good to go. Good thing I brought it."

I heard his laugh through the rocky passageway, then some faint shouts as he recruited help. I maneuvered my patient into position and told Davis to pull. They did, and Manuel slid backward, into the tunnel.

I climbed in after him. As Davis and his crew slowly dragged him across the rocks, I tried to protect his shattered legs from even more damage. When his shoulders got stuck in a narrow passage, I turned his body to get him through. I checked his pulse every so often, just to be sure he still had one. I couldn't bear the thought of getting him this far only to lose him now.

Now I could see sunlight, growing steadily brighter as we approached the outside world. We were tantalizingly close when another aftershock hit. I immediately put my arms over the back of my head and neck. After today, I would probably do it in my sleep.

The shaking wasn't that strong, but it triggered a disturbingly loud "crack" as something in the rubble above me broke. A flood of detritus poured in—shards of crockery, broken bits of furniture, all manner of smashed junk from the apartments above. It quickly filled the passageway, blocking the light. I couldn't see Manuel. I pushed through the avalanche, head down, reaching out blindly to find him.

Then another hand closed over mine. Someone else grabbed my wrist. And they were pulling me forward, into the bright, wide open day. "Are you okay?" asked a young woman in UCLA sweats.

"I think so," I said, looking at the strangers around me. "Thanks."

Then I saw Bianca, standing by the ambulance, looking anxiously into the back. I hurried over. Manuel was in there, lying on a stretcher, while Davis tended to his legs. "Will he be all right?" I asked.

"He's going to live," Davis answered. "And he's going to owe you big-time."

Bianca threw her arms around me. "Thank you. Thank you." She repeated it a few more times before releasing me.

I smiled at her. "You're welcome."

There was one more person I had to see. I found Alex in the front cab, radio in hand, listening to the latest reports. "Have you heard anything—?" I began.

"Jeff checked in with the station," Alex told me. "He's fine. He'll meet you there."

The rush of relief was like a physical force, driving the breath out of me. I heard the back doors of the ambulance close, and Alex was saying, "Hop in. We need to get your guy to the hospital."

I got in the front seat beside him. Then we were moving, lights and siren on full blast. We passed more earthquake damage. There would be a lot of work ahead. But my guy was going to make it. We both were.

About The Author

Lisa Klink started her career in the world of *Star Trek*, writing for *Deep Space Nine* and *Voyager* before coming back to Earth for shows like *Martial Law* and *Missing*. She has also written two issues of *Batman* comics and the *Borg Invasion: 4D* attraction in Las Vegas. Lisa has recently ventured into the novel universe, with three books in the *Dead Man* series published by Amazon. She is also a five time champion on *Jeopardy*, ending her run with an ironic flourish by missing a Final Jeopardy question about Women Authors.

Check out Lisa's *Dead Man* novels on Amazon:
                    http://amzn.to/1i3dGE2

"Suzie ~~Homemaker~~
Apocalypse Ass Kicker"
by Pang-Ni Landrum

"Faster! Faster!" screams the frantic Beverly Hills-bred woman sitting in the threadbare passenger seat of Suzie's late 90's minivan.

If Suzie weren't so fond of Jenn, she would clock her. Even after everything they've been through in the last hour, the woman still looks as though she walked fresh off a photo shoot. Then again, if it weren't for Jenn, Suzie wouldn't be zipping through the Hollywood Hills escaping from a horde of rabid zombie-fied animals.

♦ ❖ ♦

Suzie knew she should've said no last Friday when, at their morning workout (aka, the-kids-wreak-havoc-in-the-gym's-daycare-while-the-moms-hang-at-the-juice-bar-getting-their-caffeine-on) Jenn uttered those two dreaded words: Book. Club.

"It'll be fun!" she had said. And meant it.

Much to Suzie's hermit-favoring chagrin, her friend had yet to be wrong when it came to planned excursions—from traipsing the city on walking food tours (eight doughnut shops in three hours!) to sunset margarita horseback rides (drunk on a mountain trail!).

On the outside, their pairing makes no sense. Jenn works full time, gets weekly facials, and eats vegan, while Suzie's a stay-at-home mom, hails from (gasp) The Valley, and slow-cooks ribs that would make the most jaded cowboy cry. They both lack a tolerance for assholes, however, and that's a bond for life in Suzie's book.

"Plus," Jenn had said that morning, "the hostess is besties with the head of the preschool we want Holden to get into."

Oh, no. She did NOT just play the kid card. "Not to mention," admitted Jenn, giving her best puppy-dog eyes, "I really don't want to do this alone." Dammit.

"Look out!"

Perfectly toned and spray-tanned arms thrust out from behind Suzie and grab hold of the wheel. The minivan swerves violently. She regains control. Suzie whips around to the bottled blonde with strategically placed highlights and exposed roots sitting in the backseat, "Amber, what the fuck?!"

"You almost hit that coyote!" screamed Amber.

Better it than us. An inhuman screech grows closer. Amber whimpers and asks, "What do you think happened to the others?"

Suzie, face unreadable, "I don't know."

Suzie never imagined the end would come in the form of a needy squirrel. The night had begun with six women. Now just Jenn, Amber and Suzie remain. Not through any fault of Suzie's. She'd told the others to run.

From the manicured lawn of the Mediterranean mini-palace, Suzie took in the majestic view of downtown Los Angeles as she fidgeted with the cotton maxi dress that clung uncomfortably to the sweat forming under her cleavage. It was the only outfit she owned that strategically covered her tattoos. Well, most of them. The tail of the rising phoenix that snaked up her shoulder still peeked out from under her cap sleeve. For Jenn's sake Suzie wore her hair down, hiding her razor-shaved temples and dyed purple streak. She was in Bel Air, after all. She didn't want to scare the natives.

She had even donned pearls. Not real ones, of course, but close enough.

Rustling in nearby Oleander bushes startled Suzie and made the hair on the back of her neck stand on end. She knew she was being watched. More rustling.

"Probably just deer," surmised Amber, the aforementioned literal backseat driver and owner of the modest McMansion. She flashed Suzie an overly-collagen-injected-lipped smile. "But that's life up in the hills, right? That's why Ted and I love it here. We like being one with nature."

Suzie nodded, "I could tell by the three Escalades in your driveway."

Suzie veers past abandoned cars on the debris-filled canyon road. Next to her, Jenn repeats the Lord's Prayer under her breath, while in the back a nervous Amber bleats. As Suzie turns off Mulholland, she thinks about her husband and kids. She wants to believe they're sleeping in their beds, blissfully unaware. Safe. Suzie needs to see them. To hold them. She needs to get home. Now.

Suzie guns the minivan—a vehicle not conducive to gunning.

THUD!

"What the hell was that?!?!" Jenn yells.

Something heavy now hangs on to the car's side panel door next to Amber. It tears at the vehicle's outer shell, "It's trying to break in!" she cries.

Thick, blackened nails rip through the metal, creating a large opening. Amber screams. Something furry, something bloody with blazing red eyes hisses back as it attempts to claw its way in.

Suzie felt the women's stares upon entering the marble-lined hallway, her clogs silent amongst the cacophony of Louboutins, Choos and Blahniks.

Air kisses. Faux smiles.

Only Jenn's urgent hand squeezes prevented Suzie from bolting.

After introductions—Suzie couldn't keep them straight, they were all variations of the same woman, one somehow thinner than the next—Amber gushed to the others, "And this is Suzie. She brought a cobbler!"

The tall one, Brie? Feta? Some kind of cheese, piped up, "I hope it's organic."

Oh, it's organic all right, Buster organic-ed all over that peach tree.

But before Suzie could open her mouth, Jenn answered for her, "She made it with fruit from her backyard."

"How quaint," replied the cheese one.

There's that word again. Quaint. Like she was some fucking tchotchke they'd buy at an overpriced seaside tourist trap antique "shoppe."

Katie, the red head with the unfortunate boob job, asked Suzie, "Are you planning on making us something tonight?"

It took a moment for Suzie to realize she was referring to the knitting needles poking out of her bag, "No, I always have these with me in case I need to pass the time."

"Well, I hope you don't plan on using them tonight. We wouldn't want to bore you!" cackled Katie.

Too late. "Must be nice knowing how to knit your own clothes," chimed Addie, the Brit, another skinny beauty whose face emitted an unnatural dewy glow. Knitting is not same as sewing, asswipes.

But Suzie didn't bother explaining. Or telling them that knitting beat the hell out of her hands. Or that it was an excuse to bond with her disapproving grandmother. The old hag might have appeared frail, but she was a nasty, withholding, vengeful bitch.

"Well aren't you quite the homemaker?" Amber mused. "You make your own clothes. Grow your own food. Don't tell Ted you do any of this or he'll start getting ideas."

"Your husband shouldn't have ideas?" Suzie inquired. Another hand squeeze from Jenn. Hard.

Suzie swerves the car, trying to knock the revolting brute from the minivan. The hissing what-appears-to-be-a-raccoon still clutches to the side door. Jenn grabs the nearest object and heaves it towards the savage creature.

"Not my Birkin!!!" cries Amber. Her plea goes unnoticed. The enormous bag grazes off the rodent and flies out the door. "No!!!"

The unaffected putrid critter bares its sharp, crooked teeth.

"I don't have time for this shit" mutters Suzie.

Suzie jerks the wheel sharply again, aiming the minivan toward a row of bushes just off the asphalt. The force flings off the crazed animal. When Suzie peers at the side view mirror, she sees the determined son-of-a-bitch still clinging on; its feral jaws clenching the running board.

Dammit.

The wild-eyed raccoon dives through the hole in the door in one swift move. His mouth open wide. Bellowing an Amazonian war cry, Jenn jumps into the backseat and jams her four-inch heel into the beast's nasal cavity. Its death wail pierces the night as it releases and disappears into the darkness.

Suzie's impressed. She may have to give Stilettos another try.

♦ ❖ ♦

The women gathered in Amber's perfectly decorated library. It displayed the right lamp, the right table, the right chairs... the kind that hurt in all the wrong places.

Suzie looked around, bothered by a faint but persistent wheezing sound just outside the house.

"Oh, that's just Bob," Amber assured her, "he's our neighborhood squirrel. Poor little thing's always looking for more food. Don't worry, he'll find his way to Felix's stash through the cat door. That's why we keep the laundry room door closed," Amber cheerily winked. Suzie somehow managed to not vomit.

Then, instead of discussing one word of that miserable tome Suzie had forced herself to read while stealing five minutes on the toilet (the only respite when one's home with toddlers), Amber presented Addie the Brit to the others.

"As most of you know, Addie here is an aesthetician--"

So that explains her freakish dewy glow.

"--and the two of us arranged a little something special for tonight."

Held breaths. Suspense. "Surprise! It's a botox party!" Squeals of delight. Suzie glared at Jenn, who shrugged, then mouthed back, "Pre. School." Dammit.

Suzie needed a drink. She turned to find Addie blocking her path, botox needle in hand, expectant. An enthusiastic Amber, who stood next to Addie, gushed, "I'm telling you, it's a total lifesaver. I swear you'll thank me for this."

Doubt it.

"No. I'm fine," said Suzie. "You really should consider it," offered Addie. "Jowls are no girl's best friend."

The minivan crests the hill. In the distance, on the vast and dark Valley floor, they see a neighborhood of twinkling lights. Electricity. Signs of life. Suzie and Jenn exchange relieved smiles. Suzie just needs to get them past Ventura Boulevard.

Behind her, a dejected Amber stares out the back. She brightens, "My Birkin! I see it! It's still on the car!"

Both Suzie and Jenn interject, "Amber, no! Leave it!" "Are you fucking insane?!"

But a determined Amber peers out the open side panel at her bag miraculously caught on the back runner, "You don't understand! It's saltwater crocodile! You know how long that wait list was?"

Amber leans her weight out the door opening. Her fingers outstretched, "I can still reach it. Just. Another. Inch. Closer."

"Ow!" exclaimed Katie, the enhanced redhead.

"Hold still!" reprimanded Suzie.

The two stood in Amber's laundry "facility," which was bigger than Suzie's kitchen and living room... combined. Katie cutting her finger while slicing an under-ripe strawberry had given Suzie the perfect excuse to leave the insipid Botox-injecting spectacle.

Katie noticed her bloodstained skirt and pouted, "It's ruined."

Suzie had been mid eye roll when a loud hacking distracted her.

Felix the cat had feebly crawled in from outside and was now heaving on the cold, speckled, granite floor. Suzie could tell something was off. Katie, however, could not, "Oh, you poor thing."

"I wouldn't get too close."

But Katie didn't heed Suzie's warning. Bent over and caressing the struggling cat, she didn't notice the mangy squirrel that popped through the cat door. Or the next one. Or the next. Their pupils all similarly red and dilated.

Alarmed, Suzie grabbed Katie's hand, "We've got to get out of here." Katie looked back to the injured feline, just as Felix opened his eyes. Angry red pupils like the others. And in an instant, fangs bared, Felix leapt onto Katie's neck and chomped down. Katie howled in fear and pain.

Suzie grabbed a nearby iron and bashed it against Felix's head. Nothing. She pummeled him again. And again. Finally, his jaw slackened and let go. Katie collapsed, blood oozing from her punctured neck. Armed with spray cans of starch, Suzie jumped in front of the woman's slumped body.

Before Felix and his mangled backup crew of deranged squirrels could lunge, Suzie unloaded the cans of their contents into the animals' eyes, giving her the ten-second opening she needed to flee.

On her way out, Suzie pilfered nearby toilet bowl cleaner and bleach and dragged Katie from the room. But Suzie knew, judging from the telltale arterial spray splattered against the dryer, that Katie wouldn't be waking up.

Suzie keeps her eyes focused on the winding canyon road ahead of her. She doesn't dare look in the rear view mirror, dreading the outcome.

A scream forces her to glance behind her.

To Suzie's surprise, Amber's still alive, Jenn the only thing saving her from becoming another piece of road kill. But Jenn's grasp on Amber's ankles is slipping.

"Give me your hand!" Jenn shouts to Amber.

But Amber's still determined to save her bag, "I can almost grab one of the handles!"

"Seriously, I'm losing my grip!" Jenn warns.

Amber doesn't cave.

From the dense brush, a snarling, barbaric varmint, a former opossum perhaps, darts toward the opening. Seeing him, Suzie yanks the wheel to the left. The creature bounces off, but not before taking squealing Amber with him.

Addie had just applied the final touches to Amber's freshly-botoxed forehead when a blood-soaked Suzie rushed back into the library, dragging the lifeless Katie behind her. Whatever her name, the cheese one—Gruyere? Gouda?—shrieked, startling the others. They all gasped upon seeing Suzie.

"Oh my god!"

"What happened to Katie?"

"Are you okay?"

Suzie couldn't speak, winded from the short run. Dammit, why hadn't she and Jenn actually worked out when they met at the gym?

Catching her breath, Suzie finally managed to say one thing, "RUN!"

That was when the others noticed the howling, hissing, and mewling that seemed to surround them. They huddled together, a whimpering, nervous mass.

The noises around them intensified. Suzie and Jenn locked eyes. Grim agreement. The scratching and clawing were coming from inside the house.

Shit.

The lights went out. The women anxiously watched as the entire hillside leading into West Hollywood fell dark. Attempts at cell reception failed. No signal.

"Amber, where's your land line?" shouted Suzie.

"Who still has a land line?"

A high-pitched scream from Addie, "Something just ran across my foot!"

"Everyone to my minivan. Now!" Suzie ordered.

"We're all going to die!!!" cried Amber.

Not all of us, Suzie thought. Some of us, yes, but not all.

◆ ❖ ◆

"Amber!" Jenn screams.

Suzie slams on the brake. Reverses. She backs the minivan to be parallel with the bruised, blonde-haired mass in the street. The lump moves. Amber's alive.

Jenn and Suzie exhale, relieved.

"Amber! Get in the car, before it returns," Suzie yells. A dazed Amber sits up, scared, yet victorious—her Birkin bag back in her clutches.

Jenn reaches out for her, and just as Amber takes her hand, three feral squirrels, their red eyes ablaze, leap onto Amber's head.

"No!!!" cries Jenn.

Amber falls back onto the street, her outstretched hand helpless against the barrage.

◆ ❖ ◆

Using the glow from their smart phones, the women slowly made their way towards the front door.

Naturally, Amber had to live in such a big ass house, Suzie thought. One thing was certain: she would never attend another book club. Preschool be damned. Holden would have to learn Mandarin from Chinese take-out menus like everyone else.

From a dark corner of the entrance, a disfigured fur ball possessing the most heinous smell landed on Jenn's back.

Not waiting to find out what it was, Suzie whipped out her knitting needles and struck. Neck. Eyes. Soft tissue. When it came to gutting animals, she was swift. The creature fell away with a sickening splat.

Suzie then pushed Jenn and the others toward her minivan in the driveway.

"Wait, I've got GPS!" countered Brie-Feta. "My Mercedes is just parked on the side!"

"No, we must stick together!" shouted Jenn.

But the cheese one and Addie were already gone.

Amber didn't noticed—too concerned that Suzie had squeezed out the entire bottle of toilet bowl cleaner behind them. "What the hell are you doing to my floors?"

Suzie ignored her. "Get to the car. NOW." While Jenn grabbed a protesting Amber and ushered her through the door, Suzie poured out the bleach on top of the toxic toilet cleaner.

The trio exited, coughing and sputtering, before the noxious fumes from the combined chemicals overwhelmed the house. As they ran for the minivan, they heard squealing from the suffocating creatures trapped inside.

The three piled into the vehicle. Suzie started the car. "What about the others?" asked Amber.

"They made their choice," said Suzie.

They had made their choice. She couldn't waste time worrying about them. Suzie had to get home.

♦ ❖ ♦

Jenn and Suzie can't watch as the vermin feast on Amber's face.

Seizing their opportunity to escape, Suzie hits the gas. The car stalls.

"Go, go, go, go, go ... " urges Jenn, her eyes never leaving the creatures a few yards from the hole in the ravaged side panel.

Suzie turns the key. The minivan doesn't start. She turns it again. And again. Another pump of the gas pedal. The engine continues to make an awful choking sound, refusing to turn over. They're stuck.

"Dammit!" she yells.

Hearing the commotion, the rabid squirrels stop indulging on Amber's face and turn their attention to the minivan.

Jenn clutches Suzie's hand as the animals approach.

Even though Suzie continues to turn the key, she closes her eyes, praying for a swift end, but then ...

"Look! They're slowing!" says Jenn.

Suzie sneaks a glance. The beasts take a step and collapse. One spins in circles, the other two sway, sluggish and confused.

Suzie and Jenn exchange baffled looks.

Suzie takes in Amber's bloody, contorted body splayed in the middle of the street, then notices the remnants of Amber's prized, wrinkle-free forehead now lodged in the teeth of the woozy critters. Suzie gasps as realization strikes.

No fucking way. It's the Botox.

As the engine finally turns over, Suzie peels the minivan away from the dying, diseased squirrels. As Suzie and Jenn continue down Laurel Canyon into the Valley, Suzie shakes her head and smiles.

Amber had been right. Botox was a lifesaver after all. And, Suzie, indeed, was thankful.

About The Author

Pang-Ni Landrum, a recovering Big 10 mascot and daughter of an Asian tiger mom and a Southern military cop dad, has written on both comedy and drama shows including *Malcolm in the Middle* and JJ Abrams' *Six Degrees*. She has sold pilot scripts to Sony, Touchstone Television and E! Aside from developing for television, she co-founded SeaGlass Theatre in Los Angeles, and writes/produces *The Aftermooners*, a micro web series that exposes what love really looks like after the honeymoon phase.

Follow her on Twitter: @pangni

Check out Pang-Ni's micro web series "The Aftermooners" at: www.funnyordie.com/theaftermooners

"Positive Symptoms"
by Lauren LeFranc

I t's minus fifteen degrees and the wind's picking up. I shout for Richard, but there's no answer. He left to collect samples near the crater forty minutes ago. I try him on the radio, but it's dead. The electronics always go first when a large storm is coming in. I know that I should move, find Richard, and tell him about the woman.

I look down at her. At least a foot of ice encases her body. She must have been frozen here a long time. Her eyes are closed and her skin is almost transparent. She has a peculiar expression on her face. Almost like a smirk. What's so funny, I wonder.

A man's voice breaks through on my walkie.

I reach for it, "Richard, can you hear me?"

Static.

I try again, "Richard."

Nothing. Was he trying to tell me to wait for him? Or find my way back to the research hut? My body tightens. This storm is going to be a bad one. Mount Erebus is beautiful but violent. It already took this woman's life. I cannot allow it to take mine too.

I wonder if she was at peace when her body expired. Regardless, she was alone. I inch closer to the ice and make her a promise, "I'll come back. I'll find you again."

And then, for a brief second, her eyelids flutter. I stagger back. *No. That's not possible.* The earth groans in the distance, followed by a sharp creak. The ice below my feet trembles and spiderwebs out. I move to run, but lose my footing and fall. It's the last thing I remember.

I come to, unsure of how much time has passed. A sharp pain hums in the back of my head. I feel for it and find blood on my fingertips. I grab for my pack, but it's gone. I start to panic. I scan the landscape for any identifying markers, but the world looks invisible. I cannot tell the difference between the horizon and the ground. I whirl around in search of my own shadow. But there's nothing. I'm in the middle of a whiteout, and if I don't get back to the hut soon, I'm going to freeze to death.

A faint glow in the distance moves toward me. Its radiance attacks my eyes. I wince, but out of it I see the silhouette of a figure. He moves quicker than I'd expect, as if he's drifting above the snow. "Richard. Thank god."

But as he gets closer, I see the outline of a body that does not match Richard's. It's slighter, more feminine. And out of the whiteout walks the woman who was trapped in the ice, now free, wearing the same strange smirk on her face.

A curious ache shoots through my hands. My heart beats loudly in my throat. What the fuck is going on? This woman is dead. Moments ago, she was entrapped in ice, and now... Now, I cannot move. I cannot breathe. I can only stare.

She is less than five feet tall and certainly not more than a hundred pounds. Her eyes are as dark as her long, matted hair. She has scars across her neck. Or perhaps they're tattoos. Whatever they are, she carries them well. Animal skins barely cover her body. Her arms are strong, her stomach taut, her hands and feet the size of a child's. But she is not a child; she is very much a woman. Seemingly from another time.

I should run. But where can I go? I cannot tell up from down. I momentarily lose all feeling in my body. It's at least thirty below now. *Wake up*, I tell myself. The wind agrees, and charges at me. *Wake up*, it screams. *Fucking move. Don't let this woman near you.* But the cold seeps into my insides.

The woman reaches out and grabs my hand.

"No," I mutter. "Stop."

She obeys.

I came to Erebus for isolation. Now all I want is to be back in the hut with the eleven other researchers. I think about Richard and hope he made it back safely. I can imagine he and the others sitting around the stove, playing Monopoly, or reading. Or perhaps Mary Anne is baking one of her weird cakes for the group. She loves baking cakes.

Here I am, in the middle of a whiteout, completely lost, with a woman who is probably dead, thinking about cake.

She reaches her hand out again, and this time I take it. I'm not sure why. Her body is warm, which I failed to notice the first time she touched me. I inspect her hands – calluses along her palms, dirt under her fingernails. A moment passes and she peers into my eyes. A calm washes over me. And then, very suddenly, she reaches out and touches my face. I'm terrified, unable to move.

She points toward what I think is the sky, and tugs at my hand. She wants me to follow her...

If I believed in God, I might think she is an angel sent down from Heaven. But I stopped believing in God a long time ago.

◆ ❖ ◆

I held the paper booklet my grandparents made at Kinko's tightly in my hand, and ran my thumb across the Xeroxed photograph of my mother. She was younger and had different hair. There were at least four other pictures I knew she would've preferred, but I didn't have a say. My grandparents made all the arrangements themselves. I was only twelve. Below my mother's smiling face was a cheesy quote about birds and souls and being set free.

My mother never took me to church or talked about religion, so I knew it was one of the many things she didn't believe in. I understood why. Everything in church smelled old and seemed intentionally dismal. Even their most optimistic hymn, "Christ Is Risen," about a man who came back from the dead, sounded terribly sad. I felt guilty for not believing in any of it, but I also knew that if my mother were with me, she would've agreed. There was nothing about this service that represented her.

My grandparents didn't know that her favorite songs to sing along to in the car were The Bangles' "Manic Monday" and Peter Gabriel's "In Your Eyes". They didn't know that she didn't mind crumbs in the bed as long as they were from cookies. They didn't know that she smiled even bigger when someone said something hurtful. They didn't know that she did the best she could.

The booklet with my mother's picture on it was made of cheap, thin paper. She deserved card stock. The paper's edges didn't even line up.

It was a rushed job. I unfolded it, laid it flat across my lap, aligned the corners to match, and then folded it again. *There.* I could feel people's eyes on me. I glanced to my right and caught the attention of a gaggle of women. They cocked their heads to the side, as if to sigh in unison, *Oh honey.* I knew very little about pity, but in that moment, I decided to hate it. As soon as I turned my attention elsewhere, they began to whisper.

"Her poor kid. Looks just like her too. I always knew there was something, didn't you?"

"Well, she certainly hid it less and less."

"She was beautiful, I'll give her that. But such a mess."

I noticed a tiny piece of cracked wood coming off the edge of the pew. I rubbed my finger against it, hoping I'd get a splinter. But it wouldn't take. I wondered why these friends of my mother's decided to share their opinions on a day intended to celebrate her life. If all they wanted was to be heard, then why whisper at all?

I had to get out. I leaned over to my grandmother, "I'm going to the bathroom."

She nodded, "Do you know where it is?"

I bumbled over the kneelers in the pew, and made it into the aisle. A few stragglers were standing in the back, blocking my exit. They squeezed my shoulder on the way out, which I assumed was the most a stranger could offer in a moment like this. If they had known me better they might've given me a hug. I would've preferred that no one touched me at all.

Once I made it to the lawn I took a seat and a deep breath. Freedom, I thought. Freedom from the dusty pews, the creaking floors, the whispers; freedom from my mother's dead body enclosed inside some stupid box.

I lay down in the grass and looked up at the sun until my eyes stung. It felt good. Then I noticed something on my hand – a ladybug. I thought it was bizarre to be granted good luck on the same day as my mother's funeral.

"Meryl. Do you know what this means?"

My grandmother had found me.

I shook my head no.

She smiled, "It's a sign. A sign that your mom is still with you."

And without even thinking, I shook the insect from my hand.

I am running out of time. I can feel it with every step. I watch the breath escape my mouth and the cold air eat it up. I've been following this woman for miles, and still, there's nothing.

I stumble over my words. "Where—where are you taking me?"

She continues into the storm without answering.

Every detail on her body looks human; the follicles on her face, the small hairs sticking up on her skin. I wonder if she blushes.

Perhaps if I cut her open I'll know if she is real or not. At least then I can study her. I can have evidence to confirm my fear. Richard would understand. It was for research, I'd say. It was only for research. The woman looks back at me for a moment, as if she knows what I am considering. Then she continues through the snow, neither cold nor exhausted.

My body aches. Three different places in each knee hurt. At least I can still feel my knees, because I have lost feeling in my fingers and toes. I try to breathe life into my hands, but my lungs are too cold to offer any.

I'll be dead soon. And then I will be the woman someone else finds in the ice. Maybe I am already dead. I am, aren't I? I must be. This explains it. What a terrible heaven I've created for myself.

But I know death is not the only explanation. Not for me. It's not even the most likely. I know what this woman is. I have known it all along. Why try to make it back if the truth is only going to follow me?

With this singular thought, I allow my body to collapse to the ground. The snow hugs me, and I feel warm. This is it.

♦ ❖ ♦

It was a warm night when I smiled at her, and she stared back with a gleam in her eyes that screamed adventure. She tilted her head back and laughed. My mother did that a lot. It was always the loudest, most infectious laugh too – the kind that turns heads in a movie theater. When I laughed it always felt small, contained. As if I were holding back.

She took me out to dinner at our favorite spot because it was a Tuesday, and she said Tuesdays were more fun when we didn't treat them that way. I asked her if I could order the fried chicken breast. It was toward the bottom of our plastic menu, which meant it was one of the more expensive entrees.

"Sure," she said. "But only if you tell the waiter you want the fried chicken boob." She laughed again.

"Mom," I groaned with a smile.

She leaned in, as if we were making a special pact. "Do we have a deal or what?"

I gave a rebellious nod. She made everything thrilling.

After dinner, she held my hand as we walked home. She reenacted the waiter's reaction to the word "boob" with impassioned exaggeration. *Boooob, he said. Boooob.* Her version of the story was always better. But as we continued down the half-empty streets, her grip tightened around my hand. A panicked squeeze.

"Mom?"

Her head frantically jerked around.

"Mom? What is it? What's wrong?"

She mumbled to herself.

I looked around, but no one was there. It was happening again.

She tugged on my backpack and yanked it free from my shoulders. She unzipped the center pocket, reached inside, and found my purple scissors. The same pair I used to make construction paper snowflakes that morning.

This was not the first time my mother saw things that weren't there. She was sick, and it was getting worse. I knew that much. But we were a team, and I made her a promise. If grandma and grandpa asked, I would tell them that everything was fine, that things weren't that bad. I decided that it wasn't a lie if I believed it too.

She cowered in a corner and clenched the scissors defensively.

I reached down to her, "Mom?"

She swung the scissors at me, "No. No. No."

I backed away. The mischief in her eyes, her big, bellowing laugh, it was all gone. She was tiny and fragile and angry. I wanted to fix her. I wanted to understand. I decided that if my mother was afraid, then I should be too.

I closed my eyes. Nothing that I had seen in this world rattled her, so whatever tormented her must have come from a world outside of our own. I imagined a gigantic, misshapen creature. It had black eyes and long, pointy fingers, like the one from that movie I saw when I stayed up past my bedtime. The creature loomed over her small body with wicked intention. *No. Stop. Please.* But these were only thoughts in my head, not words I could express. She needed my help, but I couldn't move. I tasted vomit in the back of my throat. Regurgitated dread. I screamed, but nothing came out.

The creature was inches from my mother's face, taunting her. She gripped the scissors, took a breath, and stabbed a hole in its chest. The creature's heart was bigger than she expected, but she kept at it, snipping away until it was completely torn to pieces. I smiled. She did it. She was a hero.

But when I opened my eyes, I saw my mother's body on the ground, the scissors still in her hand.

The creature took her on a Tuesday. It was only a matter of time until it would come for me.

I lie in the snow, content with my decision to die. But the petite woman standing over me does not approve.

"Leave me alone," I mutter.

She takes my arm.

"No!" I scream. "I don't want to. Leave me the fuck alone!"

She begins dragging me across the snow. I try to pull my arm away from hers. I try to dig my heels into the ground. I want to be an anchor, but she's far stronger than me. My arm is going to dislocate any second.

I beg her, "Let me go. Please."

But she won't. I feel the wet snow sliding down my back. Behind me my body is creating a path like a plow. The woman pulls harder, dragging me even faster now.

I make pictures in my head – the sun hitting my face, dancing to one of my favorite songs, making a cannonball into a pool, a marionberry pie, a good kiss, the taste of something new. I'm going to die. And that's okay.

Then the woman lets me go. I wonder if I'm falling, but when I open my eyes I'm still lying in the snow. The woman is gone. I have a strange desire to call out for her. But before I can, someone says my name.

"Meryl." A hand reaches down and touches my forehead. I look up and see Richard standing over me.

I try my best to speak, but all I can mutter is, "Where...?"

"You made it back. I need to get you in the hut. Come on." He puts a blanket over me and tries to help me up.

"Where is she?" I ask softly.

"Who?" Richard looks around, confused. "Is there someone else with you?"

I turn away from him, embarrassed, and look out into the distance. I strain my eyes to find the difference between the horizon and the ground, but everything looks the same.

And then, I see her, staring at me from afar – the woman who dragged me to safety instead of tearing me apart. I am all she has. I am the only one who sees her, and the only one who ever will.

About The Author

Lauren LeFranc grew up in Orange County, California before hipsters called it The O.C. and when most only knew it as "that place between LA and San Diego." She later attended Brown University, where she wrote and performed in the school's premier sketch comedy group, Out of Bounds. After graduating with a degree in Anthropology-Linguistics, Lauren worked as a brand strategist at the advertising agency, TBWA\Chiat\Day in San Francisco. She moved to Los Angeles soon after, and has been lucky enough to write for various dramas with her writing partner, Rafe Judkins, ever since. Lauren's credits include *My Own Worst Enemy*, *Chuck*, and *Hemlock Grove*. She is currently a writer-producer on Marvel's *Agents of S.H.I.E.L.D.*

Follow her on Twitter: @LaurenLeFranc

"Dangerous Stars"
by Kam Miller

E rika Harlow, PhD – February 13, 8:07PM
Dr. Erika Harlow knew the hush of death. She'd felt it since
she'd arrived at this scene, like the house was holding its breath.
Despite the familiar activity of the uniformed police and crime scene
technicians, an eerie feeling climbed up her back, whispered in her ear,
confirming: *This place has known violence.*

As she moved up the oak staircase to the second floor of this
restored Washington, D.C., row house, the feeling intensified. It
reminded her anew of the violence that had visited her own home
when she was just six years old.

Now a psychologist for the Victims Assistance Center, she'd been
called in on an apparent suicide. Erika took in the scene. The dead girl
lay on the flooded bathroom tile floor. At 16, Angela Dunn was 90
pounds dripping wet. Her lips blue. Her skin leeched pale. Her
drenched pink cotton sweater stained crimson at the cuffs. Careful T-
incisions marred the teenager's wrists. An X-Acto knife gleamed dully
beside the claw-footed bathtub. Bloody water nearly filled the tub.
More blood-tinged water covered the bathroom floor.

Erika felt the hallway carpet squish beneath her foot. Instinctively,
she stepped back, having violated the now-sacred tidal pool. Still she
felt its pull, its undertow. She shook it off. Erika wasn't here for
reflection; she had a job to do. She'd been called in to speak with
Angela's family – her latest foster family, the Becketts.

According to Angela's Child and Family Services file, the Becketts
had been Angela's longest placement at 18 months. In fact, Angela's
13-year-old half-sister, Claire, had just been placed in the Becketts' care
as well. So why would Angela decide to end it all now?

Erika frowned. Something else didn't sit well with her. Angela's prune-y fingers had been perfectly French manicured. Cyanotic blue showed through the pale pink base, giving Angela's nail beds a purplish hue. The precise, white tips of her nails stood out starkly as a vanity against death. The manicure offered Erika's first solid clue all was not as it appeared.

◆ ❖ ◆

Detective Carter Hunt – February 13, 7:10PM

They got the call-out during dinner break. Carter Hunt had been eating at his desk. His partner, Edison James, a 20-plus-year veteran, had vanished, going God-knew-where for his meal. All Carter knew was it wasn't with him. Carter had brought a sack of fast food back to the station house. It was better than eating alone at Mickey D's.

Crumpling the remains of his burger wrapper and stuffing it into the cardboard French-fry sleeve, he chucked the grease-stained trash into his trash can. Captain John Decker strode out of his office clutching two message slips in his hand. A sturdy man in his 50s with a gray flattop, Decker's bearing screamed former military, as did his no-bullshit demeanor. After eyeballing the bullpen, he let out a visible sigh and headed toward Carter.

"Where's your partner?" Decker asked.

"Break. I reckon he'll be back soon. We got a case?" Carter answered, his Southern drawl stroking and stretching each word, each syllable.

Washington, D.C., was technically in the South, below the Mason-Dixon line. But Washington, a veritable island of international importance, remained its own entity. The District of Columbia was a metropolis where the most powerful political players on the planet did their dirty work. This was Carter Hunt's beat. But it wasn't Carter Hunt's world.

This Carolina transplant had just been promoted to homicide detective at the Metropolitan Police Department. His colleagues made no bones about how they felt. They thought he was a country-music-loving, tobacco-spitting, Ford-F-150-truck-driving, dumb hick straight out of *Deliverance*. Well, they were wrong. He wasn't dumb, and he'd never seen *Deliverance*, though he got the gist it wasn't flattering. And the rest? Well, Carter couldn't deny he enjoyed a big truck, a little Rascal Flatts, and a pinch of Skoal.

Captain Decker ground his Nicorette gum between his molars as he studied Carter.

"We got a case?" Carter asked again, turning a palm up to accept one of the message slips.

Decker pursed his lips, then looked at the two slips of paper in his big paw.

"Suicide in NoMa," he said as he handed a slip to Carter. "Find your partner. Check it out. Write it up." Decker turned. He held up the remaining message slip and called over the bullpen, "Mancini! Anyone seen Mancini? Tell him he's up."

Carter watched Decker and the other case, almost surely a homicide, walk away. He slid his finger across the face of his phone and called Edison.

Forty minutes later they were in the car heading southeast to 4th Street toward NoMa. Edison apparently hadn't seen the need to rush his dinner on account of a teen deciding to take a warm bath in her own blood. Carter clicked through the details on the car's mobile data terminal. The girl, Angela Dunn, was in a foster care situation. The foster father found her, dragged her out of the tub, and called 911. EMTs pronounced her on the scene. Carter and Edison arrived shortly after 8PM to an already active scene.

As he slammed the unmarked sedan's door, Carter cursed under his breath. A suicide. Mancini and his partner, Strucko, got the homicide. If Edison had been in the bullpen, Decker would've given them the murder. Carter just knew it. But no, they got the suicide.

Edison didn't mind. But then, Edison never seemed to mind anything. His lined mahogany face was a map Carter couldn't read. He couldn't tell if Edison actually cared about their cases, much less the world. Carter knew this was only their third case together – the first a domestic dispute gone predictably sideways, the second a tweaker who'd punted his baby girl like a football. But Edison didn't make it easy, like he didn't want to get attached to a partner, like he was short-timing it. Or maybe Edison just didn't like him. Carter studied his partner's profile as they signed the crime scene entry log.

"How's it looking, Radar?" Edison asked the uniformed police officer managing the entry log. The nameplate on the officer's big uniform jacket read Mark Radon. He was mid-20s, fresh-faced in the cold air, yet comfortable in his own skin. Carter judged he'd been on the job for four years, maybe straight out of college.

"Cut and dried," Radar said. "DB's on the second floor. Family's in the kitchen. Oh, and the VAC's here."

"VAC?" Carter asked.

"Victims Assistance Center," Radar answered, looking at the log. "Oh, *you're* Detective Hunt. Huh."

Before Carter could answer, Edison interrupted, "Who's here from the VAC?"

"Erika. I mean Dr. Harlow," Radar said. Carter noticed Radar's face flush. Even more telling, one of Edison's eyebrows shot up.

"Come on," Edison said, heading into the row house. This was the quickest Carter had seen Edison move. Edison's knees crackled in protest as they mounted the front steps.

Outside, the red row house was squeezed between two other tall, skinny houses, each a thin cake slice of the expensive, gentrified block. Carter followed Edison into the Becketts' house.

Inside, the long, narrow home had been completely remodeled with hardwood floors, sleek finishes, and an open staircase. The contemporary furnishings – all chrome, leather, and odd angles – seemed out of place to Carter. When he'd learned this was a foster care family, he imagined a more middle-class vibe.

Edison and Carter, still in suits and overcoats, grabbed Tyvek shoe covers and purple Nitrile gloves from cardboard dispensers. Carter bent smoothly and looped the shoe covers over his shiny, black duty boots.

"Who's this Dr. Harlow?" Carter asked.

"Trouble," Edison said, stooping to pull the shoe covers over his loafers.

"Trouble how?" Carter asked.

"She's perceptive," Edison said, in his cryptic manner. Carter wasn't sure if that meant he himself wasn't trouble and therefore not perceptive. Then he realized if he didn't know, maybe he *wasn't* all that swift on the uptake. His face burned with his private realization.

Edison climbed the stairs, careful to stay to the outer edge of the risers. He pointed out the water droplets still beaded on the wooden stairs and the smear of blood on the handrail.

As Carter mounted the top step, he looked down the length of a hallway. Rooms angled off to the right. Near the center of the hallway, light spilled from an open door. Like a movie set, crime scene techs had assembled portable scene lights that blasted light through the door onto the star of the scene – the body.

The extreme light on the room threw shadows down the hallway. A woman stood just outside the glow. She cradled her elbows as if hugging herself. Her head canted to one side, implying curiosity or deep thought. Her dark purple knit dress hugged her curves. Carter noticed she was leaning into her cocked hip, giving her posture a questioning air.

Her hair, a black mass of long, thick curls, cascaded over her shoulders and down her back. It looked irresistibly soft. Carter's fingers flexed, craving to grasp a hank of her hair, to crush it in his palm, and release its scent like fresh grass or fall leaves.

This had to be Dr. Erika Harlow. Someone he would be working with, Carter reminded himself. Surprised by his reaction, he mentally shook himself from a fog of hormones, pheromones, and just plain moans. She was an unexpected being. He watched her silently. As if drawn to the lighted room, on the verge of a breakthrough, Erika stepped forward.

The beige carpet had a watery outline where overflow had soaked into it. Reflexively, she stepped back, looking at the floor.

Carter noticed the line of Erika's calves as they ascended into the secret depths of her dress. She wore black leather shoes with a modest heel, just enough to give shape to her legs. Thin leather straps looped around her ankles like chokers. Carter couldn't quite articulate why, but those straps were undeniably hot.

Ahead, Edison dodged the water trail and approached Dr. Harlow.

"I already see that look on your face," Edison said. "Don't make this any more complicated than it has to be." He watched as Dr. Harlow turned. Her face matched the rest of her – delicate features framed with a strong jaw. Her lips quirked up, a hint of amusement.

"Detective Edison James, Valentine's Day is tomorrow, so I know you don't have a hot date tonight," she said.

"You never know, I gotta stay one step ahead of Alma – that woman's still got fire in her soul," he said.

Another anomaly for Carter to consider: Edison was one of the few happily married homicide detectives in the D.C. Metro PD. Somehow, despite his cynicism, he'd dodged the hollow-point bullet of divorce. Carter vowed idly to himself that he'd never get cynical, and he would never get divorced.

"So where'd all *your* fire go?" she asked, catching Edison with her gaze. Carter stared. Her eyes were so dark they appeared to be nothing but dilated pupils. Carter felt he could tip over and fall into her bottomless eyes, swallowed whole by their dark depths. Then he realized she was smirking at him.

"Trouble in paradise?" she asked, raising her chin to indicate Carter. "Where's Mancini?"

"Dr. Erika Harlow, this is Detective Carter Hunt," Edison said. Carter slipped past Edison. He offered her his hand.

"Nice meeting you, Doctor," Carter said, enveloping her small hand in his. He was careful not to squeeze it too tightly. Her eyes narrowed, really taking him in.

"Are you visiting from out of town?" she asked.

"Uh, no. Just got promoted. I'm his new partner," Carter said, confused.

"No way, you and Mayberry here are going to be a regular thing," she said, smiling past Carter to Edison.

"Apparently," Edison said.

Still holding Carter's hand, Erika gripped it more firmly. Still smiling, she stared up into his bewildered face.

"First, I know you're a big strong man, but I'm not fucking fragile. And call me Erika. Death is the great equalizer, don't you think? We'll be spending quite a bit of time around corpses," she said, letting his hand slide out of hers. "And lastly, are you two going to investigate this murder, or are you just going to write it off as a suicide?"

Edison let out a groan.

"Murder?" Carter asked.

"Don't listen to her," Edison said. "We haven't been on the scene for two seconds and she's playing sleuth. Erika, let us do the investigating and you do the consoling."

Erika's sparkling, dark eyes remained on Carter. He was curious about her claim. What if this was a murder, not a suicide?

"Come here," Erika said. She took Carter by the elbow and guided him to where she had been standing. From behind him, she directed him to look into the death room. A crime scene technician in a white Tyvek suit snapped photos of the tableau.

"What do you see?" Erika asked Carter. He felt her warmth at his back. He could swear he caught the briefest whiff of lavender over the metallic scent of blood. He pushed his thoughts of Erika down in his mind and focused on the scene.

It was a black-and-white tiled bathroom. The floor was awash with blood-tinged water. Beside the white claw-footed tub lay the body of a 16-year-old girl. Pink cotton sweater and dark leggings. The girl was drenched head to toe. Two deep T-incisions sliced her inner wrists. These incisions left red, gaping wounds like crosses set against pale skin. The bathtub was filled with bloody water. His gaze stopped on the X-Acto knife.

"Looks like she filled the tub, got in, slit her wrists with that X-Acto knife, and bled out," he said.

"Look closer," she said.

Edison stepped around to see. His shoes squished in the damp carpet, but he ignored it.

"Looks like she killed herself," Edison said.

"Do you see it?" Erika asked Carter, her presence palpable. Carter felt compelled to look more carefully. Like a camera focusing, he saw connections.

"She's clothed. Why run a bath and get in with your clothes on?" he said.

"Good," she said. Edison moved closer.

"If she was being abused, she might not have wanted whoever found her to get off one last time," Edison said, his voice quiet. "And it was the foster father who found her."

"That's true," Erika agreed. "But look at her hands."

Carter noticed her fingernails were painted in a particular way – clear with white tips. This wasn't a little girl's DIY paint job.

"She's got a fancy manicure," Carter said.

"Girls get manicures when they're planning ahead. Some important event – a date, a dance, a recital, something to look forward to. What else?"

"No hesitation marks," Edison said. And just like that they were all on the same page. For the first time, Carter and Edison were spitballing theories. They were in a rhythm, a flow, and it was all because of this woman.

"What's on that prescription bottle?" Carter asked, noting a small, clear, yellow plastic bottle lying on the floor. The crime scene tech, absorbed in her work, didn't hear him. Afraid of losing momentum, he tried snapping his fingers and pointing.

The tech swiveled her discerning glare on Carter. An eyebrow arched on her smooth, chestnut-brown face. Instantly, Carter wished he could take the whole finger-snapping, command-pointing posture back and re-record that past 15 seconds with a more tactful approach. Edison intervened.

"Ms. Finch, have you had time to shoot the scene?" he asked. She brightened at Edison's deferential address.

"Just finishing. You want to enter, Detective?"

"If you don't mind," he said. She snapped a couple of extra shots, then she sloshed out of the bathroom, her Tyvek shoe covers soaked. As she stepped out of the bathroom, she slipped off the shoe covers and tossed them into a plastic bag. She stepped onto a disposable Chub pad laid out on the carpet to dry the bottoms of her shoes.

Finch eyeballed Carter. He nodded at her and offered a half smile in a vain attempt to smooth things over. Finch pursed her lips as she slipped past Erika and Carter. Finch's womanly hips required a wider berth, forcing Erika and Carter closer together. As Erika's body brushed Carter's back, he decided the gaffe was completely worth it.

Pulling on his Nitrile gloves, Edison carefully stepped into the wet bathroom. He touched the pill bottle.

"Hydrocodone," Edison said. "The prescription is made out to a Sarah Beckett."

"The girl steals a bottle of Vicodin from her foster mom *and* decides to slit her wrists in a warm bath?" Erika asked. "That seems like overkill."

"She could've wanted to dull the pain of the cut," Edison said.

"I'd buy that if there were hesitation marks, testing her pain tolerance, but those cuts are serious," Erika said. "They were made by someone who was committed." Carter touched her arm. The knit fabric slipped easily beneath his fingertips. She looked up at him and he almost forgot what he was going to say.

"Does her toe look broken?" Carter asked. Erika turned back to the dead girl. The girl's great toe on her right foot angled off to the left. Edison examined it. Carter noticed the girl's toes matched her fingernails, a clear finish with precise white tips.

"Signs of a struggle," Edison said. "Someone holds her down in the bathtub. Drugged and half drained of blood, she fights, clawing at the slick tile and kicking to get out. She kicks her foot into the faucet hard enough to break her toe."

"She fought for her life — she fought like a girl," Erika said with reverence. Carter knew women had a special reserve; they could dig deep when the going got tough. Still, he wondered how Erika could speak with such conviction. Was it all the things she saw in her work? Was it personal experience? Or both?

"Whoever held her down is gonna have scratches all over his arms," Carter said. "Might get his DNA from under her fingernails."

"Not necessarily; there's something else," Erika said.

Carter studied the scene. Edison fell quiet, too, as he looked over everything.

"Spill it, Erika," Edison said. "What do you see?"

"There's a message across from the toilet," she said. The two detectives craned their necks to see an index card taped to the wall opposite the toilet. Carter remembered seeing Erika canting her head in this direction when he first saw her. She'd been looking at this card.

Edison read the card aloud: "Please put feminine hygiene products in the trash can. Only put toilet paper into the commode."

The two detectives turned to Erika, who waited.

"I don't get it," Carter finally said.

"Clearly they have trouble with this toilet backing up," Erika said.

"So?" Carter asked.

"Where's the plunger?" she asked.

Erika Harlow, PhD – February 13, 9:30PM

Erika sensed the new detective's outsider-looking-in nature. He was a backwoods Southerner in the District of Columbia's court. Carter Hunt was tall, like legendary Tennessee Sheriff Buford T. Pusser. The sheriff had used a baseball bat-style walking stick to mete out justice against the Dixie Mafia. She imagined Carter could handle himself in a fight. Carter could also be surprisingly perceptive, though she suspected none of his peers would pick up on this trait.

She wondered what prompted Carter to move here. Why be a fish out of water when you could be a big fish in a little pond? She guessed daddy issues. Wasn't that why all men left their homes, to escape the long shadow of their fathers?

She wondered whether father issues were at the crux of this case. Everything about it screamed abuse, and sexual abuse usually involved fathers. The detectives' working theory was Angela Dunn had been sexually abused by her foster father, Reginald Beckett, and was threatening to spill her guts to protect her sister from the same fate.

Erika had made a call and learned that another girl, who was 15 at the time, had lived with the Becketts. Soon after she moved in, she started acting out and was put back into a group home. Erika wondered if this other girl had been trying to get away from Reginald Beckett. Erika re-joined the detectives and shared the news.

Edison and Carter decided to conduct separate interviews. Erika would talk with the kids – 14-year-old Toby Beckett and 13-year-old Claire Dunn, Angela's half-sister. They likely would need the most counseling. Carter, the rookie, would take Sarah Beckett, the foster mother, and press to get something on the foster father. Edison, the veteran, would try and break Reginald.

Erika sat across from Toby and Claire in the Becketts' finished basement. Teary-eyed, Claire clung to Toby. Her resemblance to Angela was uncanny. She had the same delicate nose, fragile brow, and the full lips that bowed into a pout. She looked younger than her age, which was common for foster children. The neglect and emotional trauma in their young lives stunted their growth. Grim irony: Their stolen childhoods forced them to grow up faster than their more sheltered peers. This trauma – the death of a loved one – had young Claire grappling with feelings that many people struggle with even as adults.

Toby had an arm slung around Claire, who leaned into him for support. They sat on a turquoise couch arrayed with Nerf balls, stuffed animals, and game controllers. *Entertainment Weekly* magazines and remote controls littered the glass-and-chrome coffee table. Erika sat on a faux black-and-white cowhide ottoman with her back to a dark flatscreen TV. This was the kids' rec room – a place where they came to kick back, play video games, and shoot Nerf balls at a plastic hoop that hung from the wall. It was a place where kids could be kids – until one of them got killed.

Erika was struck by Toby. He looked oddly familiar. His blond hair was cut in a popular sling-bangs haircut often sported by skateboarders and slackers. But he was a freshman at Gonzaga High School, a highly competitive Jesuit Catholic high school, so he couldn't be a slacker. There had to be ambition behind his casual good looks. His hazel eyes picked up the colors around him. Right now, they were a striking violet from the turquoise couch and his purple Gonzaga sweater. He sniffled, wiping his nose on the back of his hand. Erika leaned toward them.

"I'm sure this has been a shock to you both," Erika said. She had to tread lightly. She wanted to find out if there was abuse in the house, but her priority was caring for the emotional well-being of Toby and Claire. "Was Angela having any problems?"

"She said everything was going to be all right," Claire said, her voice choking. "She said she'd take care of me." She buried her face in Toby's sweater. It was clear Toby and Claire cared for each other, which made the possibility of splitting them up now that much worse.

"What would be all right?" Erika asked.

"Life, I guess," Claire answered, her voice muffled. "But it never is."

"Did Angela leave a suicide note or an explanation?" Toby asked, hugging Claire tighter.

"We're still looking. Was she worried about anyone in particular? Did she mention if anyone made her feel uncomfortable? Was she in trouble?" Erika asked. Claire's face snapped toward Erika.

"Angela was perfect! She was the perfect sister! Everyone loved her," Claire said. Erika absorbed Claire's anger. She'd seen it many times before – people in pain lashed out at the ones who tried to help them. Toby rubbed Claire's arm and she subsided.

"She could be a little moody," Toby said. "One week she'd be happy, the next she'd be . . ." He let it drift, searching for a word.

"Irritable? Depressed?" Erika suggested. While these could be signs of suicidal ideation, they could also indicate sexual abuse.

"Well, yeah," Toby said, shrugging his shoulders.

"She was not," Claire said, pulling away from Toby a little.

"You weren't with her for the past year and a half," he said gently. "You just got here. I'm not saying she was bad or anything. She was just a teenage girl."

"Boys think just because it's shark week, girls get bitchy," Claire said.

"Shark week?" Erika asked.

"You know, your period," Claire said. Erika nodded, understanding. Claire looked up at Toby. "How can you say that about Angela? She loved you."

"You and Angela?" Erika asked Toby.

"No, it was nothing like that," Toby said.

"No, he took care of her," Claire said. "He took her places, bought her clothes, got her nails done pretty. He's going to take me next." Claire brightened a bit at that.

"Well, that was really nice of you, Toby," Erika said with a sinking feeling. She studied the boy. "It sounds like you and Angela were close."

"He was going to take Angela to the St. Valentine's dance tomorrow," Claire said. Her face crumpled and she began to cry in earnest as she realized her sister wouldn't see another tomorrow, much less a Valentine's Day.

Erika recalled the martyrologies of St. Valentine. The most popular myth involved a priest, who, under the reign of Claudius the Cruel, married young lovers in secret. Secrets could bond, but they could also doom. Erika needed to excavate some secrets, and she might have to get her hands dirty. She just hoped learning these secrets wouldn't be too cruel.

Toby rubbed Claire's back as she shook with quiet sobs.

"Gonzaga High," Erika said.

"Yeah," Toby said, half-apologetically.

"'Forming men for others,'" Erika said, quoting the motto of the prestigious school.

Toby shrugged.

"An all-boys high school. Must be difficult to meet girls."

"Not for Toby. He's famous," Claire said proudly.

"No, I'm not," Toby said, waving his hand as if brushing the idea away.

"Famous?" Erika asked.

"He's on TV," Claire said.

"Just a couple of commercials," he said. "And I booked a small gig on a show that shoots out of Baltimore. It helps pay for school."

Now Erika knew why he looked familiar. She'd seen him on television. He was a child actor. She wondered just how good of an actor he was.

"You must have lots of girls who'd go to a dance with you. Why were you taking Angela?"

"I thought she'd enjoy it," he said.

"What about you? Would you have enjoyed her?"

"Yeah, sure," he said.

"A freshman bringing a foster sister to an elite high school's function. That was pretty risky for your reputation – TV star or *not*," Erika said, pushing him now.

Toby's hazel eyes grew flinty. A crafty intelligence rose from within him. Erika had sensed this presence in other adversaries. It was a malicious gene, something imprinted in human DNA since our ancestors headed east of Eden. In some people it was recessive. In others, dominant.

"I might be a freshman, but my friends are sons of diplomats, senators, and CEOs," Toby said. "Class means an entirely different thing at my school."

"Why bring Angela into it? It wasn't exactly her world. In fact, it was a pretty big leap from her lowly background of group homes and hand-me-down clothes," Erika said. "Did you just want to rub her face in it?"

"I thought she might learn something. I thought she might make friends," Toby said. With a lightning bolt of understanding, Erika knew the truth.

"*You* didn't have trouble meeting girls, but your friends did. You were taking Angela for them," Erika said.

"No, it wasn't like that," Toby said, trying to regain his innocent appeal.

"Stop it!" Claire said. "Both of you stop saying mean things about Angela."

"Tell her, Toby. Tell her why you invested in that mani/pedi for Angela. Did you buy her a special dress, too?"

Claire looked up at Toby. Her eyes swam with tears.

"What's she saying? Tell her you just wanted to be nice to her. Tell her you loved Angela," Claire pleaded.

Toby's face fell. He quickly turned away from Claire.

"What? What'd you do?" Claire asked Toby.

"You didn't mean for anyone to get hurt," Erika coaxed. "But Angela did get hurt, didn't she?"

"She found out I showed her picture at school," he said. "Some of the guys thought it would be, I don't know, they called it slumming. They wanted to hook up with her."

"You were going to pimp her out?" Claire's voice rose to a wail.

Toby looked at Claire anew. He'd always seen the sweet side of the girl, but her anger suited her better. It suited a girl who had been discarded, disappointed, and dismissed too many times in her young life. Claire launched herself at Toby. The fingernails he had planned to carefully groom into enticements dug into his chiseled cheek and drew blood.

"Little bitch," Toby yelled as he shoved Claire away. He was stronger than he looked and she was small for her age. She careened into the glass-and-chrome coffee table. Her head hit the tempered glass with a teeth-jarring thud. The glass shattered beneath her as she tumbled onto the floor.

Toby touched his face; his fingers came back red. Hatred flared on his handsome features. He was an angry angel, ferocious and unforgiving. He loomed over Claire, who lay in the litter of glass shards, a field of dangerous stars. His hands balled into fists as he readied to descend on the girl.

Before he could move, Erika was on her feet and moving toward him. At the speed of thought, she'd covered the few feet between them. She planted her foot behind Toby's, the back of her calf perfectly placed for her next move. She slammed her fist into his sternum. Toby rocked backward, tripping over Erika's braced leg. He gasped for breath, still reeling from the punch. As he fell, Erika thought of Angela struggling for breath, for her life, in a bloody bathtub.

"What are you doing?" Sarah Beckett yelled as she pelted down the stairs. Carter, Edison, and Reginald Beckett followed close behind.

"Toby, are you all right?" Sarah asked, striding past Claire. She kneeled next to her son. "Oh my God, your face." Sarah turned on Erika. "I'll have your job for this."

"I don't think so," Erika said, her voice as clear and cool as a running stream.

Carter stepped toward Erika, his hand outstretched as if he were directing traffic. "Let's all take a deep breath."

Edison grasped Carter's arm.

"Watch," Edison said. And with that one word, a hush fell over the scene.

Erika locked eyes with Sarah Beckett. "When did Angela come to you? When did she tell you what Toby wanted from her?"

"Sarah, what's she talking about?" Reginald asked. He'd once been an attractive man, but something more than the years had worn him down. Erika guessed it was his wife's ambition – her ambition for him and for their son. Erika knew he was about to see ambition taken to the extreme. What would a stage mother do to protect her son from scandal?

"Tell him, Sarah. Tell him your son was going to pass Angela around to his friends. That he was grooming her for sexual favors," Erika said, never taking her eyes off Sarah, who glared back defiantly.

"That's not true," Reginald said. "Toby, tell her that's not true." Despite his protestation, doubt crept into his tired eyes. He knew his wife, and he knew his son.

"She liked it, all the attention. She wanted it," Toby said, his voice shrill. Reginald took a step back as if his son's words were fists.

Erika remained focused on Sarah.

"Angela came to you. You're the one she would've trusted. She wanted to protect Claire. She wanted you to save her, save her sister from your precious son."

"Mom?" Toby said.

"You knew you had the Vicodin," Erika said. "What'd you do? Tell her you would talk it out over hot chocolate or a cup of tea? We're going to find out in the autopsy."

"You don't have any proof," Sarah said, her voice rising at the end, questioning her own confidence.

"You drugged Angela, telling her all the while everything would be okay. You'd take care of everything. Then you ran the bath," Erika said.

"No, Angela committed suicide," Toby said. "Mom?"

"You helped her, dazed and drugged, into the tub. You cut her wrists. That was your first mistake," Erika said. The slightest question touched Sarah's brow. Erika raised her voice now. "Hey Radar, why don't you show us what you've found?"

Sarah's eyes darted toward the basement stairs, but Erika continued.

"As Angela was bleeding out, she came to. She fought, so you held her down with the first thing within reach, the toilet plunger. We're going to find bloody water in her lungs. Aren't we, Sarah?"

Sarah's eyes flicked to her son, then her husband. She looked like a cornered animal.

"You treated Angela like a piece of shit, like she was something to flush away," Erika said.

Radar walked downstairs carrying two evidence bags. He shot a glance at Edison, who nodded. Radar lifted a sealed bag containing a white-and-green plastic toilet plunger with a green rubber end. Claire's face lit with recognition. So did Toby's.

"That was in the upstairs bathroom," Claire said. Then she turned to Sarah, "You killed my sister?"

Erika stepped between Claire and Sarah. With a look, Erika warned Claire to wait.

Radar handed the bagged plunger to Edison.

"We found this in a nearby dumpster. You can see it's stained with blood," Radar said.

"Sarah?" Reginald asked.

"We also found these gloves," Radar said.

Radar held up the second evidence bag. Inside were dainty yellow rubber kitchen gloves with garish red fingernails painted on the outer tips. Their kitschy nature made them that much more obscene. Edison took the evidence bag from Radar. He studied the gloves.

"I bet they'll light up like neon at a rave once we hit it with Luminol," Edison said.

"I want a lawyer," Sarah said, struggling to hold on to her defiant edge.

◆ ❖ ◆

Detective Carter Hunt – February 13, 10:25PM

Carter closed the unmarked sedan's door. Sarah Beckett sat in the back seat, handcuffed. The night hadn't turned out the way he'd expected. A suicide turned into a murder and he'd met the first person who made his life easier. Someone who created a rhythm between him and his partner. A woman Carter wouldn't mind creating a rhythm with himself.

He scanned the dispersing scene. Angela's body had been removed. The crime scene techs were packing up. Officer Radon was pulling down the crime scene tape. Edison stood on the front stoop talking with a bewildered Reginald Beckett.

On the street ahead, Erika crouched next to a car door. Claire Dunn sat inside listening, waiting to be taken to Child and Family Services. As the car started, its exhaust spewing a cloud of vapor in the chill night, Claire flung herself into Erika, hugging her, holding on as if she were a lifeline. Carter imagined Erika seemed like the only haven in this tempestuous world. And in his own way, he knew how Claire felt.

Erika had shown him that he and Edison could be partners. Battle-hardened yet empathetic, she had pushed them to look beyond the shallow surface. She made him feel less alone, less a stranger in this strange land.

Erika stood and watched the car take Claire away from this trauma. Claire would be assigned to yet another new group home. Maybe she'd get placed in a foster family. Maybe she wouldn't. Once the car was out of sight, Carter watched Erika's shoulders sag.

Then, almost as if she sensed she was being watched, Erika turned and pinned Carter with her coal black eyes. As she walked toward him, he felt her pull. He met her half way. She hugged her arms to her body for warmth. Carter wanted to envelope her, to pull her to him. He remembered the brush of her body against his; it left an impression, a desire for more.

"That was pretty amazing what you did," Carter said. He immediately wished he was more articulate.

"It doesn't change the fact Angela Dunn is dead, or that her sister is going back into the Russian roulette of the foster care system," she said. "Together, those two girls belonged to each other. Now Claire will always feel singular." She looked up at the glare of the starless city sky; it still seemed foreign to Carter.

Erika's words and the light-polluted sky magnified Carter's loneliness. That's what he'd been feeling since he'd moved to D.C. – singular. Identifying the emotion tempered it.

"How'd you learn to fight like that?" he asked. A sly smile snaked across her face.

"Girl's gotta have her secrets," she said.

In that moment, Carter wanted to know every single one, every detail. He studied her as she turned her attention to the Beckett house. Violence had changed it into something ominous. Its Victorian Gothic exterior loomed over them. Its double windows were haunted eyes. Toby looked down from one of those windows. He was a ghost. He was a demon. He was a teenage boy.

"Wish there was something we could get him on," Carter said, staring up at the boy.

"Don't worry. You'll see him again. He's his mother's son."

"When we will we see you again?" Carter asked, the boy forgotten for the moment.

"D.C. is populated with people who do bad deeds," she said, her breath fogging with each exhalation, hanging like a promise in the air. "Something will bring us back together soon. 'Night, Detective."

As Carter watched Erika stride away, the city under the starless sky seemed navigable for the first time.

About The Author

Kam Miller is a TV writer who has created pilots for FOX, CBS, 20th Century Fox, Paramount Television, and Universal Cable Productions. She wrote for Fox's *Killer Instinct* as well as the long-running NBC show *Law & Order: SVU*. Her first feature, *The Iris Effect*, was produced while she was at the USC School of Cinematic Arts. Currently, Kam is developing several TV projects as well as novels. For more with the characters Erika Harlow and Detective Carter Hunt, look for Kam's novel, *Myth of Crime*.

Follow her on Twitter: @kammotion

You can also find her online at "Glass half-full in Hollywood" at kammiller.com.

"Home"
by Jess Pineda

S omeone once told me, "Turbulence is like pothole in the sky, unexpected, but really no big deal." Well. It's 2005 and I'm three Xanax deep, in a tiny, vibrating plane to Cuba and it totally feels like a big deal.

The flight jolts again and I feel that acidy deliciousness slide up and back down my throat. Wonderful. Where was my damn intuition when I booked this flight? Riiiight, it was telling me to experience the world. To give back. To, for once, step outside my comfort zone. Huh.

As it turns out, I do not enjoy being uncomfortable.

We shift to the left and a very hairy young man is thrown against me so hard that I can smell what he had for dinner three nights ago.

"This has got to stop," I say aloud. The hairy guy mumbles an apology.

"It's not you, it's me," I assure him. (It's totally him.) "I'm going to go talk to the pilot and see what's going on." (Also I don't like the smell of fennel.)

"I don't think you're supposed to do that..."

But I wave him off. This is a humanitarian trip to help the needy in Cuba. Everyone on the plane is here to do good. The very least the pilot could do is stop flying like a moron.

"So, hey, guys. I'd realllllly appreciate it if you'd, you know, chill out with the crazy flying because it's making it a little hard for me to breathe. See I have these things called anxiety attacks, and every time you pretend that this plane is a bouncy house, a little part of me dies. Right there... and here. Wait for it... and there it is again."

"Do you know that it's illegal to come to the flight deck?"

"I thought this was the cockpit?"

"It's the same thing."

"I don't understand."

"Ma'am, please return to your seat. We will be landing soon."

"Does that mean you'll fly better?"

"Get back to your seat."

I start to turn away but... "Sooooo is that a yes or a no?"

"Get back to your seat or I will have you arrested when we land."

Rude.

When the steamy heat of Havana hits me in the face I feel like I'm finally home. I take a deep breath in ... maybe this is the place that I'm supposed to be, maybe that plane ride was worth it. I feel great, so great ... until the native Cuban girls point and whisper "Americana" as I step out of the airport. I guess my disguise of clean, newish clothes didn't fool anyone. I pass a man standing outside a run down port-a-potty selling toilet paper for 25 cents a square. And of course, the *policia* carrying a large and very loaded gun doesn't speak any English. When I tell Mr. *Policia* I'm looking for my group, *Viva America*, he points to a tattered billboard of President Bush in a gas mask, "Terrorist" written on it in large red letters. Suddenly I feel like a foreigner in a land that's my own.

Before I left on the humanitarian trip I was given a little rundown on Cuba: everyone here makes what is equal to eight American dollars a month. That's right, the Starbucks latte and scone you're currently enjoying is worth more than a doctor's monthly salary. But Cuba believes that its inhabitants are just fine. They don't need any humanitarian assistance. Tell that to the man selling toilet paper.

A man comes up behind me and softly says, "Yennifer?" I nod and he smiles. He's round and short and points to his shirt, which reads only *Viva*. Through makeshift Spanglish and laughter I guess that he's the guide for our group. His name is Tato and he's sweet, but nervous, as the *policia* watches on carefully. Cuba is very much not America. Freedom not included.

Tato will be driving me and a few other volunteers around the city for the duration of the trip, but right now it's just him and me. I offer to take the wheel, trying to immerse myself completely in my new old hometown. "It's not safe for me to drive yourself," he tells me. "Is it safe for you to drive me?" He doesn't answer.

We arrive at my hotel, Ambos Mundos, which I'm thrilled about, as it's known as Hemingway's hotel. Hemingway loved loved loved Cuba and in this particular hotel he wrote the first few chapters of *For Whom the Bell Tolls*. I try to invite my guide into my hotel for dinner but he politely declines. I offer to pay, of course, but he says no. I push the subject and he gets very nervous. He has to go. I think people here are really weird. Until I get inside the hotel.

It's run-down but still beautiful in the way ruins always are. The crumpled buildings tell stories of life, love, and loss. I meet up with another young hippie-ish girl in her twenties, Vanessa, who's here to volunteer for the same organization. She tells me quietly that she's brought a suitcase full of clothes, Tylenol, and an old laptop to donate along the way. She's done this trip before. And while I'm in Cuba to broaden and better understand myself, she actually came here to help. AKA, I'm the worst. I ask her about the guide and tell her how resistant he was to come in.

She smiles, "You have no idea, do you?"

I shake my head.

"Remember the days when "Colored People" had their own establishments with backdoor entrances? Well, the Cuban government thinks that certain restaurants and hotels are only to serve government and tourists."

"Why didn't he just tell me? How can that even be legal?"

"Welcome to the wonderful world of communism."

And that was only the beginning.

The next day we awoke early and got ready to go on our first mission to an orphanage. I thought that I would be able to truly relate to these kids. I was abused as a kid (oh, hey, Xanax) so I knew what it felt like to be alone and hurt. But I wasn't prepared for anything I would experience. I expected a sprinkling of lonely kids, used toys, bunk beds...

What I found were children living in the sewer.

The actual sewer. Underground and filled with rats and drugs and human excrement. I dropped down into the dark, damp, shitty-smelling sewer and my flip flops landed in what I'll call "mush" for those of you with soft stomachs. The smell was so overwhelming that I wished myself back to the plane. But alas, I was here. For worse or for worser.

Our flashlights bounced up and down the murky circular hallway as we called out, "Hello? Hola?" both hoping and not hoping we would find someone. We searched the halls for anyone, really. It didn't have to be a kid. Sometimes women would flee from abusive husbands, men would hide from the government, but more often than not, it was the children who made the sewer their safe place. It seemed like hours before we came upon exactly what we were sadly looking for.

A little boy.

Maybe nine? I couldn't tell from where I was standing, but he was skinny and dirty and scared. He shivered when he saw us, then bolted. Like fast. Nine-year-old boy fast. Everything started happening in slow motion. The others in the group ran past me but I stood stock still. My heart thumped faster and faster, my palms dripped with sweat, and I was dizzy. So dizzy. I knew was having a panic attack. A big one. In this moment of action, all I could think about was myself. Why wasn't I running toward the helpless child? Why was I just standing here? Why couldn't I make my feet move?

I reached in my back pocket to pull out my emergency Xanax. Shaking, I folded back the tissue that covered the drug I so needed. I went to pluck it up, but my trembling hands weren't up to the task and I fell through my hands onto the sewer floor. "No. No-no-no-no-no!" I went to scoop it up but the tiny tablet had been dissolved by the water and muck. I was left alone with my fear. My pulse raced. Silence. Spinning. And then black. All I saw was black.

I woke up dazed, the world a blurry mess. Tato's kind face steadied before me. "Had a little too much to drink, eh?" Ah, that Cuban sense of humor. It's funny how hard times bring out the need for hard laughs.

I look to my left and see the young boy showered, but still scared.

"We pulled you two kids back here. One was heavier than the other but I'm not making any accusations." Tato winked.

"I'm so embarrassed," I mustered in my own broken Spanish. "I swear I'm so much better on Xanax. My life is a mess." I drop my head in my hands.

Vanessa kicks my shin and nods toward to the small shivering child next to me. Right. This one wasn't about me. I reach out to touch the small boy, but he backs away sharply and covers himself, blocking what's left of his body from an expected blow. The woman who runs the orphanage, Gloria, knows this all too well and offers the boy a tattered blanket. He doesn't dare move. She says that it's been a big day for him. We should go. We all did great work today. A life was spared.

I wanted to do so much more.

The next day we went to Pinar del Rio to feed the elderly. A solid enough mission, and thankfully this time I didn't pass out, but I kept thinking about the young boy I failed. I had to go back to see him. So, when we were done, I packed up half my dinner and asked Tato to take me back to the orphanage.

"Should I bring a fainting bed this time?"

"Better safe than sorry," I smiled. Maybe I was getting the hang of their tragic comedy. I pocketed my Xanax before we left. I wasn't feeling *that* funny.

When we got to the orphanage I smiled and hugged a few of the other kids. The little boy, now known as Juan, sat in a corner quietly playing.

"Hey, Juan." This time he looked up at me. "I brought you some of my dinner. Do you want to go to the kitchen to eat it?" No response. Gloria said that he hadn't eaten all day. Every time they tried to offer him food, he'd put it on the plate of another child, not wanting them to go hungry. Even at that young age it seems that he knew there is never enough to go around. And this kid who had absolutely nothing wanted to give away everything.

In my broken but already way improved Spanish, I re-approached the tiny hero. "Juan, this food is for you. I saved it because I liked it so much and wanted to share it with only you. I'm going to put it in the kitchen. You can eat it whenever you want, okay?" Juan didn't respond but stared at me, right in the eyes, before returning to his toys. I looked to Gloria and she nodded. I really wanted to hug him, but I refrained. I know all too well what it feels like to be scared.

The next night I wrapped up half of my dinner again and dropped it off for Juan. He didn't take the food from me directly, but Gloria told me that he must've gone to the kitchen in the middle of the night and eaten because the box was gone. I felt like I'd won the lottery.

The rest of the week went quickly. Each day we set off to help in another way. We drove through the mountains to Valadero Beach, where you could walk in the clear water for miles and it wouldn't pass your knee. There we delivered vitamins and Tylenol. On another day we dropped off a used laptop to a college student. We also gave a struggling family a microloan so that they could start a bicycle taxi business. Not to make it about me, but to make it about be, I found that I was so wrapped up in doing good that I didn't have time for an anxiety attack. Maybe it was because I didn't have time to let my mind worry, but I think it was more that I just didn't let it worry about me.

Every night I'd had the same ritual, taking half my dinner to my new friend, Juan. He'd stare up at me with those giant brown eyes and not say a word. He wasn't ready for a full conversation. And I was okay with that. I knew pushing him wouldn't help, and I just wanted to let him know I was there.

On my last night, I stayed a bit longer.

"I want you to know that I have to go back home tomorrow, but if you're up to it, I'd like to remain friends. Would you like that?"

The usual response, nothing but solemn dark eyes stared back at me.

"You don't have to decide now. But I did bring you some final dinner. Drum roll ... " There was no drum roll, only raised eyebrows. Oh, my American humor. "Okay, no drum roll, but this you will love. I consider it a delicacy. I present to you ... " I unveiled a big square box. "Pizza!" I waited for applause ... it didn't come. I added, "I heard they made the best pizza in Chinatown, so I got the biggest one I could find specifically for this occasion." He looked at me quizzically. "It's all for you." Again, I desperately wanted to hug Juan, but instead I smiled softly into those big brown eyes, and turned to leave. I had almost gotten to the door when I heard the very specific creak of a pizza box. It's always been one of my favorite sounds in the world, but today, it sounded like angels singing. When I looked back I saw Juan's tiny frame had been completely enveloped by the box. Childhood at its greatest. I stood there, heart and eyes overflowing. I had gotten this kid to eat pizza!

I sat back down with Juan, his eyes as big and round as the massive pizza pie in front of him. I watched as he picked up piece after piece, savoring each bite. When he was finally done, he took the box to the other room where the rest of the children sprawled about and dropped it off for them. My work here was done.

I got up to leave once again, but as this time I felt a tiny tap on my leg. It was Juan.

"Gracias, amiga." (Thanks, friend) he said before he hugged me. HE hugged ME!

I imploded with love. If this is what it was like to do good, it's no wonder Mother Teresa hung around for so long. I hugged him back so hard I thought I'd shatter his bones. I held on until he was ready to pull away, wanting him to get all the hug he needed. After a few minutes, he let go. I wanted to leave him with some words of wisdom, but all I had was myself, so I did the best I could. I bent down and looked him in the eyes. This time, my Spanish was perfect.

"I want you to know that you are not just special, but spectacular. I don't have to tell you that life isn't easy, you already know that better than anyone, but you need to know that you have a choice. Everyday. You can choose to be scared of how big life can be, to take it sitting down, trembling in fear. Or, you can choose to run towards this big scary life, with everything you have, so fast that fear cannot catch you." I paused. "It will be scary, and at times you won't believe you can get through it, but in the end, on the other side there is something spectacular. For me, it was you. For you, it was pizza."

Juan smiled, "I like pizza."

"And I like you." I returned his smile and reached in for one more hug.

I left my address and phone number for Juan to get in touch with me should he want to. He promised that he would.

◆ ❖ ◆

Early the next morning I was on the way to the airport. It had been only a week in Cuba, but that week had given me a lifetime of change. I said goodbye to my new friends and waited in the ramshackle, air-condition-less airport for my tiny plane to arrive. I thumbed around in my pocket and found my Xanax. I should have breathed a tiny sigh of relief, but what I felt instead was a twinge of good ol' Catholic guilt. Was I really going to take these meds after I had given that whole speech to Juan about fear? I mean, no one would know except me, so who cares, right?

Except ... *I* would know. And somehow on this trip that little thing called integrity snuck itself into my psyche and wouldn't leave. If Juan could suffer through all he had and been okay, I could figure out a way to survive life and the fear it brings without medication.

So, I found the nearest bathroom, locked myself inside a stall, and had a funeral for my Xanax.

"Thanks for all the good times. Well, I guess they weren't really good times. It's actually been pretty terrible ... you know racing to the hospital thinking I'm having a heart attack, the overwhelming feeling that at any given second I'm gonna die, the blackouts ... this has sucked. And thus, it's time for me to say goodbye, old frenemy."

And with that, I flushed my Xanax down the toilet.

I boarded the plane feeling really confident. I can do normal people things! All of the normal people things! Driving, walking, and even flying! Look at me go in the airplane! Wheeee! Just like a real grown up!

Until the pilot announced over the loudspeaker, "Ladies and gentlemen, please buckle your seatbelts, we're about to go through bit of moderately severe turbulence."

There were many things I had a problem with in that speech. One, there were a total of 10 people on this plane. The pilot did not need to use a loudspeaker. He really could have just yelled over his shoulder. Second, moderately severe? It's either moderate or severe. Make a decision, dude. And third, turbulence. Or rather, TURBULENCE?!?!?!?!

I was not prepared for this outcome when I flushed the tiny pills of wonder down the porcelain cup of doom. What was I going to do? I would certainly not survive this plane ride. For sure, 107 percent, I was going to die. The plane started rattling back and forth harder and harder. My soul jumped out of my body every time we hit a bump. My lungs felt like they were squeezed by a panini press, my palms sticky and wet, and my heart was beating so fast that it didn't feel like it was beating at all, more like one continual thump or hum that buzzed in my chest. Blackness clouded me, I was ready to give into the dark. But then, I heard a child's cry.

It came from the seat right behind me, where there was a small boy, about eight or nine years old, tears streaming down his face while he screamed in Spanish.

"I don't want to die!"

I knew exactly where he was coming from. Others on the plane were starting to get scared, too. The pilot was focused on the task at hand and therefore unable to assuage our fears as he was doing his job. In contrast with my first flight to Cuba, which was just a few bumps, this one was actually in danger. As we shook and dropped and I swear we even spun upside down, I saw people throw up in brown paper bags, luggage fall from the overhead and worst of all, this poor child's screams. He was all alone, no adult on the plane with him, and terrified. My pulse continued to hum, and I was no less scared, but I had to make a choice. I couldn't get off this plane, but I could make it better.

"Help! Please God!" The little boy shrieked as we dipped again. I turned around in my seat.

"What's your name?" I yelled into his screams.

"¿*Como?*" His tearstained face and wild eyes broke my heart.

"Your name?" I said in Spanish. "What's your name?"

"Hans."

That took me by surprise. "Really? Hans? That's not a Cuban name." The plane shifted hard to the right and both Hans and I hit the side panel. The rest of the plane gasped. Right now was not the time to discuss his parents' unique choice of names.

I turned and faced Hans again. He was sobbing. "Hans?" He didn't look up, he was starting to hyperventilate. I put my hand on his knee. "Hans? Have you ever been on a plane before?"

Hans managed to shake his head, "No."

"Where are your parents?"

"America."

It took me a second. Why was this kid alone on a plane while his parents live it up in the States?

"Mama won the lotto. Now I go," he managed between sobs.

This doesn't mean what you think it means. To Cubans, winning the visa lotto is like a get out of jail free card. It's a chance to go to the US with not only the proper paperwork, but it's done for free. Freedom for free... sorta. Often this freedom means that the one lotto-wining parent will travel to the US, without their children, to try and make a better future for them. They can petition for their children to come with them, but it often takes years.

"When was the last time you saw your Mom?"

"I don't remember, I was only two."

It had been at least five years since he had seen his mother. If my heart was broken before, it was shredded now. But I didn't have time to feel sad. The plane continued to shake, and Hans was terrified.

"But I will never see her again. We are going to die!"

The plane rattled again as if to answer, yes.

"Okay Hans. We are not going to die."

"Yes, we are! Look how scared everyone is!"

"Hans, have you ever been on a rollercoaster?"

"We don't have them in Cuba."

"Right ... " I searched my brain, "But maybe in a movie? Have you ever seen a rollercoaster in a movie? The kind where people go so fast they throw up their lunch? But they ride it again and again because it's so much fun?"

"Yes! One time in an American movie about baseball, there was a rollercoaster and all the kids threw up! I've always wanted to ride the rollercoaster until I throw up!" Hans smiled the tiniest smile.

The plane tilted. Hans' eyes were fearful but he was no longer crying. The rest of the plane had quieted a bit, and somehow, the person most terrified of flying was distracting them.

"Yes! Exactly. I have an idea. Let's pretend we're on a rollercoaster. So every time we feel a little turbulence, we laugh."

"What if it's a really big scary bump?"

"Then we raise our hands as high as they'll go and say 'Wheeeeee!'"

As if on cue the airplane tumbled. I forced myself to laugh. It sounded a slightly hysterical but Hans bought it. He forced a smile too. Our aircraft shook a few more times, each time we'd laugh harder, our laughter breaking the residual fear.

Our pilot came over the loudspeaker, "We are beginning our descent. As we come through the clouds, the turbulence will rattle us a bit more so please keep your seatbelt tightly fastened."

I looked back at Hans. "Okay, that means hands up! Ready?"

He smiled. This time, it was anything but tiny. "Ready!"

The turbulence increased and we started to hit those hard dips that remind you of your last meal. Every time, instead of screaming with fear, we squealed with delight.

"Wheeeeeeee!" Hans and I both laughed as we dropped.

The rest of the passengers joined in on our adventure, raising their hands as we continued to shake and sway in the air. Before long we were approaching the runway. As soon as the wheels hit, the entire plane erupted into applause. Sure, it was partly because we were so happy to be there alive, but also because we made our thrill ride, well, thrilling. We literally laughed in the face of danger. And though danger put up a good fight, we won.

When I stepped off the plane this time I was changed. I had figured out who I was, but only when I realized it was not about me. This whole, beautiful and terrifying life was never just about me. It's about eating pizza. Riding rollercoasters. And reaching out to others in my most inconvenient time. Because that's when they, and I, need it most.

About The Author

Jess Pineda was born and raised in the sweltering Cuban heat of Miami. While in college, she worked undercover in Cuba, transporting medical supplies and micro-enterprise loans on behalf of an NGO. When she decided she was done with being a "good person" she threw all their crap in a car (including her husband) and moved to Los Angeles to be a Television Writer. Since then, Jess has worked on shows such as *The River*, *Zero Hour*, and *Workaholics*, and even had a short stint as a dolphin trainer at the Seaquarium. If you want to contact her and tell her how pretty she is you can do so on the Twitter.

Follow Jess on Twitter: @thejesspineda

"Stolen Child"
a *Daughters of Lilith* story
by Jennifer Quintenz

Come away, O human child!
To the waters and the wild
With a faery, hand in hand,
For the world's more full of weeping than you can understand

—"The Stolen Child" by William Butler Yeats

She could have been a marble statue in my arms, each miniature feature carved with exquisite care. But this little statue was warm, her beauty made even more perfect by the life flowing through her. Even in the darkness, her skin seemed to radiate a precious glow. She sighed and shifted in her sleep, and my heart swelled. Pain and pride and fear made a jumble of my thoughts. *Vulnerable. She is too vulnerable.* I frowned. Only five years old. If I couldn't get us out of this, she might not live to see six.

I leaned back against the wall of our sanctuary. It was slick with moisture and grime, but I was too tired to care. The old storm drain access tunnel wouldn't have been my first choice for a safe haven, but Emlyn had been exhausted. She'd never had to run like this before; she didn't understand what was happening. I couldn't bring myself to tell her that the life she'd known these past five years was over. But I could give her rest. And so we'd stopped running. I'd pried a metal grate up out of the street and told her to hurry, slip inside. She'd peered down into the darkness, and then those wide, gold-green eyes turned back to me. Fear shone from her face, but she swallowed it, knelt at the edge of the hole, and grabbed the first rung of the ladder tightly. Little hands, still plump with baby fat, curled around the rungs as she lowered herself into the unknown. I'd scanned the street, and then—satisfied our hunters hadn't seen us—slipped into the shaft after her.

Darkness was nothing to me. If anything, the lack of light clarified my world. I could pick my path easily through the blackness, but Emlyn was still a child. For her, the darkness fell like a veil over her eyes, blinding her to her surroundings, just as it had for her father. A human weakness. It would be more than ten years yet until Emlyn began to experience her Lilitu gifts. For now, I would have to scout the darkness for both of us.

Emlyn shivered, and a faint whimper escaped her lips. A nightmare? I scanned the tunnel, torn. I'd heard nothing in the hour that we'd been hiding here, but that meant little. Guardsmen were persistent. Once they realized we'd slipped their net, they'd double back. Just the thought of their return made my skin start to crawl. We needed to *move*. We couldn't afford the luxury of sleep, not if we hoped to see the dawn. The Guard was not known for its mercy. Capture would mean my death; Emlyn herself was living proof of my crimes. And as for Emlyn? They would not care that my daughter was innocent of any wrongdoing. To the Guard, we were both Lilitu demons. Succubae. This conflict traced its roots back to the beginning. It mattered little to the Guard that Adam and Lilith were both created from the same clay in Eden. The Sons of Adam and the Daughters of Lilith had been at war since the day Lilith left Adam alone in the Garden. We preyed on them. They hunted us. End of story.

Emlyn whimpered again. A wave of anger surged through my gut. She needed me, and here I was cowering like a feeble human. Nothing stirred in the tunnel. I pulled in a long breath, weighing the risks. But then Emlyn shuddered, and my resolve failed. A few moments couldn't hurt. I closed my eyes and slipped into her dream.

Emlyn stood at the edge of a precipice. Her eyes were squeezed tightly shut, her little toes digging into the dirt at her feet. The earth around us was scorched, black and lifeless. The landscape seemed eerily familiar. I suppressed a shiver. She'd never seen the Lilitu realm, and yet it could have formed the backdrop of her nightmare. Something moved through the air around us, a vague and sinister monster dreamt up by Emlyn's sleeping mind, fueled by her very real fear. At least I could end this torment.

"I'm here, cricket."

Emlyn's eyes opened. She gave a soft cry of relief and hurtled toward me, burying her face in my stomach. Her shoulders trembled. I ran my fingers through her dark hair. When she looked up again, some of the fear had eased from her face. "A nightmare?"

"That's right." I felt her arms loosen from around my waist. I caught her hands and dropped to one knee, bringing us eye to eye. "But it's over now."

"In here." Her eyes darted to the sky. "What about out there?"

I stared at her, startled. Emlyn—could she be *lucid*? It would be years before she should be able to navigate her dreams. I gave her a bland smile. "Out where, baby?"

"In the real world." At my blank expression, she sighed with frustration. "In the not-dream world. Why are those men chasing us?"

"It's—it's complicated, cricket." My eyes dropped to our hands. Her little fingers threaded between mine so naturally. How could this be wrong? My amazing Emlyn. My brilliant, funny, silly little girl. She was as much a part of me as my own beating heart. And if I'd obeyed the treaty, I would never have known her. She would never have come to be.

Emlyn tilted her head to one side, studying me closely. "I'm not a baby. Maybe you should try to explain it?" She looked so serious, that adult expression so out of place on her cherubic features. My heart twisted painfully in my chest.

"I will, I promise." I gave her a gentle smile and reached up to smooth her dark hair back from her face. "But right now you need to rest."

"No dreams?" She regarded me with a strange mixture of hurt and relief.

"No dreams," I echoed. I leaned forward and kissed her on the forehead, imposing my will on the fragile scaffolding of her sleeping mind. The nightmare slid away from us, and when I pulled back, Emlyn's eyes were closed. I released her, and she drifted, peacefully, in the formless void of dreamless sleep.

I slipped out of the bubble surrounding Emlyn's consciousness, into the vast landscape of the universal dream shared by all living creatures. Dots of light dusted the vast expanse like stars, each one a sleeping mind. I was exhausted and weak; it was tempting to slip into a stranger's dream and garner even the barest amount of sustenance. But more than energy, I needed an ally.

I focused my thoughts on Mielyn. From the dusting of stars, one gleaming mote began drifting toward me. As it grew closer, I sensed Mielyn's presence. Confident, independent, mischievous…familiar. Mielyn and I had spent a decade traveling this country together over a century ago. She was the closest thing I had to a sister, though we'd not spoken since before Emlyn's birth.

Well, what are you waiting for? I felt Mielyn's amusement. *Come in.*

I placed my hand on the shell of Mielyn's dream, and then I was standing next to her on the ramshackle porch of an old Victorian boarding house. I smiled. We'd stayed here for several months on one of our jaunts, feeding off of the male boarders in the house across the street. She looked exactly the same, down to her '20s-era blond bob and fire-engine red lipstick.

"Look at you, darling. The years have been…" Mielyn's eyes narrowed, "just wretched to you, Vy. Honestly, what did you do to piss off Father Time?"

"The Guard's found us."

Mielyn's smile slipped. "By 'us' should I assume you mean—?"

"I have a daughter." My eyes welled with unexpected tears. "We're in trouble."

"A—a daughter." Mielyn licked her lips, unsettled. "You have a daughter. Tell me she's adopted."

"She's mine. She's five years old." I brushed a hand across my eyes, smiling as the image of Emlyn crossed my mind. "You'd love her, she's a real spitfire—"

"And you're surprised they're hunting you?" Mielyn's voice hardened. "Vy, we have one rule."

"I know, but—"

"*One night.* You find a man, you feed from him for one night, and then you move on. No harm, no foul, no turning him into a hollow shell of a body incapable of independent thought. No *killing* him." Mielyn turned away from me abruptly. "I can't believe you got so—I mean, what the hell happened? You were too tired to look for fresh meat? You *know* what happens after three nights! Did you lose track of the day?"

A cold knot of anger seized my stomach. "It wasn't an accident, Mielyn. I wanted this. I wanted a child."

"Oh, well, I'm sure if you just explain that to the Guard, they'll forgive you for taking a human life."

"Mielyn, I haven't touched a man since that night—"

"You killed a Son of Adam." Mielyn glanced back at me, her expression stony. "What about the rest of us? What you've done paints a target on all our backs."

"Don't be naive," I snapped. "The Guard doesn't care how gently we treat our prey, only that we're predators. They want us all dead."

"That's not exactly true." Mielyn spoke so softly that for a moment I thought I'd misunderstood her. "What do you mean?"

"There is a Lilitu who works with the Guard."

I studied Mielyn carefully. "A prisoner?"

"An equal. They trust her. And there's more." Mielyn glanced around, as if worried someone might be listening in. She stepped closer to me, dropping her voice. "They say she's made a deal with Sansenoy."

"A deal? With an *angel*?" My voice sounded sharp in my ears, full of mistrust.

"In return for her help, he's promised to make her human."

"That's not—that can't be true."

Mielyn shrugged. "Perhaps. But I've heard it from many tongues."

"Are you saying we could—?"

"Us?" Mielyn chuckled bitterly. "When we've been in the business of deflowering strapping young men for centuries? I don't think so."

"What makes her so special, then?"

"She's young. She hasn't taken any lovers yet. But there's a line, and if she crosses it, the deal's off." Mielyn shrugged. "Just a matter of time, if you ask me."

"Emlyn," I whispered. "She's never hurt anyone. Maybe—maybe the angel would offer her the same chance?"

Mielyn's smile faded. "I kind of got the impression it was a one-time offer."

"But you don't know for sure." The possibilities unspooled in my mind. Emlyn as a human. Free from the specter of execution at the hands of the Guard. Free to love without the fear of destroying her mate. She could have a real life. My eyes refocused on Mielyn. "Who is this Lilitu? Where can I find her?"

"Her name is Braedyn," Mielyn said slowly. She gave me a veiled look, as if half-afraid I was losing my mind. "She lives in New Mexico."

"What town?"

Mielyn licked her lips again. "Vy, she lives *with the Guard*. If they find you walking their streets—"

"Mielyn, *please*."

For a moment, Mielyn didn't speak. Then she let out a long sigh. "Just promise me you'll be careful."

"I will." I caught Mielyn's hand. "I promise."

"It's called Puerto Escondido."

I opened my mouth to thank her, but before I could speak the words—

◆ ❖ ◆

—my eyes snapped open. The skittering clank of metal echoed through the tunnel. Someone had stumbled into the pile of rusted cans I'd fished out of the muck. I heard the muffled curse of a man and froze. The beam of a flashlight reflected off the water-slicked walls fifty yards behind us. The light burned in my vision for a fraction of a second before my eyes adjusted. Adrenaline flooded my system. I grabbed Emlyn by the shoulders and shook her, more roughly than I'd meant to. Her eyes flew open, and I clamped a hand over her mouth, muffling her gasp of surprise.

"It's me," I whispered. "We have to move, cricket." Emlyn's hands groped for me blindly. I caught one of them and gave it a warm squeeze, and then released her mouth.

"They found us?" Her voice trembled, even as she struggled to sit up.

"Let me carry you, baby." I stood and helped Emlyn to her feet. "One, two, three." She jumped up into my arms, encircling her legs around my waist and clinging to me tightly. My attention was fixed on the men behind us, growing closer by the moment. I started moving, picking my way quickly along the slick concrete path. I knew their progress would be halting, slowed by the limits of their human sight. We rounded a bend, and I picked up speed.

But this time, I wasn't running away. For the first time in a long time, I had something to run toward.

◆   ❖   ◆

We climbed onto the damp street at dusk. The grate let us out into an alley, looking out onto a side street. I could hear the buzz of evening traffic, but no cars passed us by. I helped Emlyn out of the hatch and then carefully replaced the grate behind us. It fell into place with a dull clang. Hopefully, the sound was too faint to carry over the noise of the storm-water runoff in the tunnels below.

Emlyn watched me, her small face smeared with dirt. I gave her a smile and bent to wipe away the grime with the edge of my shirt, discovering only then that my clothes were even grimier than her face. I let the fabric fall and glanced around. We needed to get off the street. If there were Guardsmen in the tunnels, there were sure to be Guardsmen searching the streets as well.

Light flooded an alley across the street from us. I turned. A man slipped through a door and let it close behind him. He was tall and lanky, dressed simply; black pants and a white button-down shirt, rolled up at the sleeves. He fished in his pocket for something. A cigarette. I scanned the street quickly. No pedestrians. I could see the street at the end of the block. Cars zipped past, none lingering long enough to give me cause for alarm.

"Quickly, cricket." I clutched Emlyn's hand tightly and darted across the street. I focused on the man, urging the last of my energy into the task before me. I was filthy, exhausted, and scared, but none of that mattered. In less than a minute, this stranger would be willing to die to protect us. He looked up, lighter poised just inches from the end of his cigarette. I smiled—the inviting kind of smile that makes them think they're a part of something special, something important. A faint breeze kicked up, teasing my hair back from my face. I held his eyes as we approached. Eye contact helped, and I was weak enough to know I needed to pull out all the stops to enthrall this man. He swallowed, suddenly looking unsure. The flame of his lighter flickered. Went out.

"I'm sorry to bother you." Even depleted as I was, my voice came out rich and smooth. My honey voice, Emlyn called it. Not that I made a habit of enthralling men around her, but she'd seen it enough times to know this was different than a normal conversation. "We're a bit lost. Do you know someplace we might be able to get a bite to eat and clean up?"

"Yeah—yes. I mean, please, allow me." He thrust the forgotten cigarette back into his pocket and opened the door, revealing the warmth and chaos of a busy kitchen. I felt my smile falter. Too many eyes. He saw my hesitation. "It's okay. Really. My kitchen, my rules." He knelt to face Emlyn. "Are you hungry? I make a mean macaroni and cheese."

Emlyn glanced up at me quickly, biting her lip. "Can we, Mom?"

Alarm bells raged in the back of my mind, but what choice did we have? We needed to get off the street. I forced my features to relax. "I don't suppose you've got something green to go along with that?"

The man smiled, his skin crinkling pleasantly at the corners of his eyes. He held the door open further and waved Emlyn in. "Ladies first."

Emlyn danced into the kitchen, the prospect of a warm meal making her practically giddy.

Twenty minutes later—after doing my best to clean us up in the cramped kitchen bathroom—Emlyn and I sat down at the staff table. It was a comfortable booth situated in a corridor between the main kitchen and the dishwashing area. It was loud, uncomfortably warm, and right in the flow of traffic, but I felt safer here than I had since we'd fled our apartment two days ago.

"Macaroni and cheese for the young lady." A steaming bowl of macaroni, cheese, and broccoli slid in front of Emlyn. Her eyes lit up. Our host presented her with a huge bowl of shredded cheddar cheese, ready to spoon some over her dinner. "On a scale of one to ten, how much do you love cheese?"

"One hundred!" Emlyn grinned.

"Oh! She broke the needle!" The man set the bowl down next to Emlyn. "I'd better leave this with you, then." He glanced at me out of the corner of his eye and winked.

"Thank you," Emlyn said, spooning a small mountain of cheese atop her meal.

"Easy, cricket," I warned. Emlyn gave me a sheepish smile. She pushed the bowl of shredded cheese aside and loaded her spoon with a huge bite of the creamy pasta. I felt another pang watching her; she was starving. My mind tripped over the last 48 hours. When had we last had something to eat?

"And for you, ma'am?" He turned toward me, his smile softening. With what? *Pity?* I shrugged, embarrassed to be taken for someone…fragile. "Anything."

"Really? No preferences? Steak? Lobster? Chilean sea bass?"

"Surprise me."

"All right, but you do realize that's a dangerous thing to say to a chef."

I smiled in spite of myself. "I'll just have to trust you."

"Ben." His voice was full of warm empathy.

I looked up, surprised.

"My name. Not that I expect you to reciprocate—or—I don't mean to suggest that your telling me your name would mean anything untoward." He smiled nervously and cleared his throat.

"Untoward?" My smile widened.

"Mom was an English professor," he muttered, flushing a rosy pink. "I'll just get started, then." He rubbed his hands across the front of his crisp white apron and started to turn away. I caught his hand.

"Thank you, Ben." Looking up at him, I was surprised to find I really meant it. Gratitude wasn't an emotion I experienced in a typical day. Ben smiled again, then nodded and strode back into the main kitchen.

"He likes you," Emlyn said, not raising her eyes from her meal.

"Does he?" I asked, nonchalantly.

"Don't pretend. I know what you are." She took another bite, and a drop of cheese slid down her chin.

I reached across the table to wipe it off. "Oh, yeah?"

"You used your *magic* on him," she said around the mouthful.

"So now I'm magic?" I smiled at her, trying to mask my unease. I'd tried so hard to provide her with a normal childhood. That had meant assimilating. Getting a job waiting tables. Paying for things like rent, clothes, preschool. Granted, I made out better than the typical waitress, but I only turned on my charms for the men who seemed like they could afford to tip a little extra. And even then, I'd only used my charms once or twice a week. The goal wasn't to fleece the town. We needed to make a life here. And, in front of Emlyn, I'd been *very* careful. *Not careful enough,* said a little voice in the back of my head.

Somehow, Terrance Clay had found out there was a Lilitu in this town. And as soon as one of his spotters caught sight of me outside the restaurant, it was all over. The life I'd painstakingly built for Emlyn—gone in an instant.

"Yes." Emlyn glanced around and lowered her voice. "You're a fairy."

I stared at her, suppressing a laugh. A *fairy?* Well, I guess "fairy" sounded nicer to a five-year old than "demon," but seriously.

"That's why you used to tell me that story at bedtime," Emlyn said, frowning. "The one about the crying. Isn't it?"

I racked my brain for what she could possibly be talking about.

Emlyn watched me, growing a little distraught. She set her spoon down. "With a fairy, hand in hand?"

"Yeats," I breathed. His poem, *The Stolen Child.* Will had written a few stanzas one afternoon in 1886, after we had dallied on the banks of a beautiful river in his homeland of Ireland—well before the world knew him as W. B. Yeats. I'd always found it beautiful and sad. Had I recited it for Emlyn? "Come away, o human child. To the waters and the wild, with a faery, hand in hand, for the world's more full of weeping than you can understand."

Emlyn's face eased. "Yes, that's it. I'm glad you didn't forget."

I studied Emlyn, but she took another huge bite, returning her attention to her bowl. As I watched her wolf down her macaroni, I tried to strategize. We needed to get out of town. My car was useless. They knew my address; they'd be watching my house. Buses and trains were out; they'd be keeping an eye on the stations, too. A taxicab. If I could enthrall a driver, we might manage a free ride out of the state.

With my mind fixed on our escape route, I didn't notice Ben approaching until he set a plate down in front of me. It was a large bowl of spaghetti tossed with vegetables.

"It's kind of a specialty of mine," Ben said, shrugging. "You looked like you could use some comfort food, and this has always made me feel better."

"Thanks." Honestly, I was hungry enough that I wouldn't have objected to anything. Although usually, when a chef tries to impress me, he shows up with some kind of trussed-up lamb chops or filet mignon spooned with a reduction of something or other. When I took my first bite of this dish, I was totally unprepared for the wave of flavors that washed over my tongue. "Oh." I closed my eyes, trying to identify what specifically it was about the combination of flavors that was blowing my mind. "It's good."

When I opened my eyes, Ben was smiling at me, pleased. "*Bon appétit.*" He turned and walked away, with a definite spring in his step.

Across the table, Emlyn sat back. She'd made a valiant effort to demolish her macaroni, but the bowl was still over half full. Emlyn yawned wide, eyes scrunched up tight. Watching her, it was like the years melted away from her features and I was staring—once more—into the face of my newborn daughter. But then she opened her eyes and blinked, and my newborn subsided back into the face of this smart, insightful little girl.

"Tired?" I reached across the table to smooth a lock of hair back from her face. She nodded, eyes half-lidded. "Why don't you lie down on the booth," I suggested. "Get some sleep. I'll be right here."

"Okay." Emlyn rubbed at her eyes, then lowered herself to the worn red leather of the booth's seat and curled into a little ball. It didn't take long for sleep to claim her.

I ate in silence, savoring the soft rise and fall of Emlyn's breath, the rich flavors of my meal, the warmth of the kitchen. Even the sounds of the staff and the clink of dishes melded into a pleasant white noise. I knew I should take this time to plan, to think, but instead, once I'd finished my meal, I let myself drift near the edge of sleep. Time passed. Someone cleared our table but left us alone to rest. After what felt like half an hour or so, I stirred.

The frenzy of the kitchen had died down to almost nothing. The only sound left was the spray and clink of the dishwashers in the room behind us. I looked around for a clock. It was nearing midnight. I ducked my head under the table. Emlyn was still asleep, clutching her fists under her chin. I sat back. While I couldn't shake the feeling that we'd already stayed in one place too long, I didn't want to disturb her. Maybe we'd dodged a bullet. Maybe the Guard had moved on.

Ben approached, pulling off his apron. "Is she still out?" He nodded in Emlyn's direction.

"Yes." I gave him a grateful smile. "When do you close?" I glanced back at the kitchen. It looked like the last of the line cooks were heading out.

"Don't worry about it. We should let her sleep." Ben offered me his hand. "How about a glass of wine?"

I opened my mouth to decline, then shrugged. "Sure." I took his hand and let him lead me to his wine chest.

"Are you in the mood for anything in particular?" He turned toward me, the soft glow of the wine cabinet giving his eyes a handsome sparkle. He was an attractive man. On first glance, I'd dismissed him as tall and lanky. But up close I could see that he was lean with well-defined muscles under his shirt. He smiled, and I realized he'd caught me sizing him up.

I smiled, flustered. "After that meal, I'm leaving the culinary decisions entirely in your hands."

Ben laughed and then turned back to the wine cabinet. "You know, if you two need a place to crash for the night, you'd be welcome to stay at my place. I have an extremely adequate fold-out couch."

"Ah…" I lowered my eyes, thinking. It was hard to ignore the benefits of spending a night with him. One night with this man could replenish all the energy I'd expended over the past few days trying to dodge the Guard and keep Emlyn safe. I could ensure that Emlyn slept soundly and woke none the wiser about our interlude. He was standing so close that the scent of him, the warmth of his body were extremely tempting. And it had been so long. Since Emlyn's birth, I'd been too afraid of drawing attention to our location to risk spending even one night with a man. Yes, one encounter would only weaken him, doing no lasting damage. But, still, I'd decided to play it safe and visit men for sustenance only in their dreams. Now, letting my eyes travel back to Ben's face, I found I didn't want to hurt him. That realization sent a shiver down my spine. After years of abstinence, did I no longer see men as prey first and foremost? And this man, Ben, had treated both Emlyn and me with such kindness. I shook off the thought, chastising myself. I'd enthralled him. What kindness he'd shown us wasn't real, merely a side effect of my power. And yet…

A deep sadness welled within me, something I hadn't felt in years, since well before Emlyn's birth. I'd thought I'd come to terms with this. I knew I could never have a romantic relationship, not one that lasted more than three nights, at any rate. My embrace was fatal. To let myself love a man would be to sentence him to death.

"I don't think that would be a good idea," I said softly.

Ben glanced at me, then quickly away again. "Right. Whatever you need." I'd hurt him, but better this pain than the damage I could inflict. Ben pulled a bottle off the shelf and held it out for my approval. "How do you feel about Sangiovese?"

I smiled. "Sounds perfect." Ben turned toward another cabinet, this one holding the restaurant's stemware. I forced my shoulders to relax. It was better this way.

The door to the alley burst open across the kitchen. A man strode inside. He had close-cropped salt-and-pepper hair. He scanned the various workstations, looking for something. For me. I didn't need to see his face to know who it was.

Terrance Clay.

Terror shot through me with searing fingers. Ben turned toward the intruder. I reached for his arm, but I was too late to stop him.

"Excuse me, can I help you?"

Clay turned toward him. And that's when his eyes landed on me. In one smooth motion, he drew a dagger out of his jacket.

"Whoa, mister," Ben set the wine down, raising his hands in a calming gesture. "Easy."

"Step away from the woman, sir."

"This is my kitchen." Ben walked toward Clay. He put his hand on the older man's shoulder, spinning him back toward the door. "It's time for you to—"

Clay caught Ben's arm with his free hand and turned, pulling Ben off his feet. Before Ben could regain his balance, Clay drove an elbow into Ben's stomach, dropping the younger man easily. Ben hit the ground hard, curling reflexively into a ball. I heard him gag, but I couldn't pull my gaze off Clay.

"Mom?" Emlyn's thin voice pierced the silence. I spun around, horrified. Emlyn sat up, rubbing the sleep out of her eyes, unaware that she'd just announced her existence to the enemy.

Clay's eyes flicked from Emlyn back to me. "So," he drawled with a syrupy Southern cadence. "It's true." He turned back to Emlyn, a cruel smile turning the edges of his mouth.

"Don't touch her, Clay." I crossed the distance to Emlyn without turning my back on Clay, reaching a hand out blindly behind me. Emlyn raced to meet me, grasping my hand tightly.

"I'm afraid you have me at a disadvantage," Clay said. "And I do try so hard to keep all you demons straight."

I didn't take his bait. "Don't harm her. She's innocent."

"Innocent?" His smile deepened. The casual way he said it sent a spray of goose bumps shooting down my arms.

"I'm the one you want. I'm the one who broke your treaty. She's never hurt a soul," I breathed.

"You stole a man's life for that brat." Clay shrugged, as if it were simple arithmetic. "Her birth is her crime." He walked toward us with slow, deliberate steps. I shoved Emlyn behind me, trying to preserve the distance between us, as though we weren't trapped. Ben struggled to his feet behind Clay, still woozy.

"Please." There was no reasoning with him. I knew this, and yet I couldn't stop myself. The only thing I could think about was Emlyn. She filled my head. My girl. My little girl. He was going to kill her.

"Mom?"

"It's okay, baby." I gave her hand another squeeze. "It's going to be okay."

"I'll make it quick," Clay said. "But that's all the mercy I can offer for—" Suddenly Clay dropped to one knee.

An iron skillet swooshed through the air where Clay's head had been half a second before. Ben stood behind him, the skillet clutched in his hands like a baseball bat.

"That was unwise, son." Clay rose to his feet, facing Ben.

Ben's eyes shifted from Clay to me. He didn't have to say anything. I grabbed Emlyn's hand.

Ben swung again. Clay moved, catching Ben's wrist and twisting. I didn't wait to see what happened. As soon as Clay was clear of our path, I pulled Emlyn forward, and we raced as fast as we could to the swinging doors leading from the kitchen into the restaurant.

The dining area was mostly empty with maybe a handful of patrons scattered about, finishing after-dinner drinks. Every head swiveled toward us as we burst into the room. I froze, and Emlyn clutched my hand even tighter. I picked out the Guard in an instant. There were four of them, three soldiers and a spotter. The spotter was leaning against the front door. When she saw me, she straightened. The soldiers didn't wait for her warning. They turned toward us, hands gripping weapons beneath their jackets.

I scooped Emlyn into my arms and backed away from the advancing Guard, scanning the room for the nearest exit. A soldier anticipated me, moving to block access to the emergency exit.

Clay exploded out of the kitchen doors to our right.

I felt the adrenaline shoot like liquid ice through my veins, lending me a burst of strength. "Close your eyes, baby," I whispered. Emlyn buried her face into my neck with a ragged sob. Her arms tightened around my neck at the leathery snap of my unfolding wings. This was not how I'd hoped to introduce Emlyn to our true nature. I felt a pang of regret but shoved it aside. My only task now was ensuring our survival.

"Clay, she's cloaking!" The spotter, no longer concerned with discretion, launched herself into the dining room, sprinting toward us as she drew her own daggers. But even as Clay turned back toward us, my wings enveloped Emlyn, rendering us both invisible to all but the spotter. Screams split the air as patrons staggered up from their tables, horrified.

I turned away from the spotter and ran. The dark side street was visible through a large picture window. "Hold on," I hissed, clutching Emlyn to my chest as I leapt onto a table. I turned my body, impacting the window shoulder-first, shielding Emlyn with my wings. We hit the ground hard, and Emlyn rolled out of my arms, balling her arms over her head instinctively. As soon as my concentration broke, my wings retracted, leaving us exposed on the sidewalk.

The window's safety glass rained down around us in misshapen cubes, catching and reflecting the streetlights like a spray of diamonds.

"Up, cricket. Quickly." I stood, still shaking with adrenaline. Emlyn looked up, then thrust out her hand. I helped her to her feet. Panic raged in my head, drowning out rational thought. The two of us on foot had no chance of escaping Clay and his soldiers. I grabbed Emlyn and crushed her to my chest. "You have to run, baby."

Emlyn opened her mouth to argue.

"Find a place to hide. Go. *Now*." I turned her little frame away from me and gave her a shove. She stumbled a few steps forward, into a pool of shadow, and then turned back, her hazel eyes bright with unshed tears.

"Mommy?"

"Don't look back." I turned my back on her. Up ahead, Clay and his soldiers emerged from the restaurant's main entrance. I sprinted across the street, feeling a surge of triumph when the spotter's shrill voice called out behind me.

"There! She's heading for the alley!"

I heard their boots on the pavement behind me. When I reached the end of the alley I risked a look back. Clay and all four soldiers were on my tail. I couldn't see Emlyn. *Good girl,* I thought. *Just keep your head down.*

I ran. At full strength, I could have outpaced them easily, losing them in the close warren of downtown streets and alleys with little effort. But I wasn't at full strength. Not by a long shot. And my energy was flagging. Ten minutes into the chase, I started to wonder if I'd make it. I should have quashed that thought instantly, but my mind leapt straight to Emlyn, hiding, waiting for me. What if I never returned to her? What would happen to my little girl?

I skidded to a stop, suddenly overwhelmed with the need to return to her. *Baby, wait for me.* I urged the thought to reach her. Though I'd never sent a thought to her before, I prayed she'd hear and understand. *I'm coming.*

A taxi was parked just up the street, though his fare light was off. I raced to the open passenger window. He glance up as I peered inside, struggling to infuse my voice with the irresistible charm of a Lilitu.

"Hey. I need a ride." I flashed him a smile.

The cabbie looked at me, unimpressed. "Then call a cab. I'm off duty."

Fear uncoiled in my gut, rising up, threatening to chase out all reason. I forced it down, trying once more. "It won't be any trouble," I said, shifting my weight suggestively. "I'm not going far."

"Then maybe you should walk. I'm not taking any more fares tonight." Without waiting for a response, the cabbie started his cab and pulled away, joining the traffic on the main street up ahead. I stared after him, stricken. If I didn't have the energy to enthrall a man—

"There she is!"

I spun around. One of Clay's men was charging down the street. I fled, racing toward the other end of the street. Only—they'd anticipated me again. Clay and another soldier stepped around a corner, blocking my escape. I skidded to a stop and then backtracked, scanning the area for an out. Distracted by the terror of leaving Emlyn to fend for herself, I darted into a blind alley. It took a moment for the dead end to register. By the time I realized my mistake, Clay's men were closing in. Two of them blocked the south side of the street, while the remaining three approached from the north.

An instant regret flashed through my mind. I should have kissed that chef when I'd had the chance. Even the minimal energy I could have drawn from him might have helped.

Understanding sunk in slowly, leaving a numbness in its wake. There wasn't a way out.

The Guard were taking their time, closing their net slowly. They knew they had me trapped. I closed my eyes, summoning Emlyn's face in my mind. With everything I had left, I sent the fullness of my love out to her, raw and pure and painful. It would have to be enough to last her for the rest of her life. I felt the emotion surge through me, reaching out, taking an almost physical form. Like a golden thread, it wove through the air around me and then shot away, seeking its target.

Exhausted, I opened my eyes.

"Where is she, demon?" Clay stood at the head of the alley, flanked by his team. I made no move to answer him.

Something tingled in the back of my mind. *We're coming.* It was so faint, I wasn't sure at first if I'd heard it or not. I turned my head away from Clay, trying to hone in on the voice.

"That's all right." Clay smiled faintly. "I've gotten pretty good at inspiring communication over the years."

Clay took one step forward. I heard the screeching of rubber on asphalt. Suddenly, Clay and his team were throwing up their hands to block out the lights of an approaching vehicle. The scene before me devolved into chaos. Clay's soldiers turned and fled, throwing their bodies out of the way. Clay's eyes snapped back to me, a snarl peeling his lips away from his teeth.

"Clay!" One of Clay's soldiers grabbed the older man and threw him back, away from the alley, away from me—and out of the path of the white van that skidded to a stop at the mouth of the alley.

The door was standing open, revealing the van's empty interior. No. Not empty.

"Get in!" Emlyn. Emlyn was there, in the van, calling to me.

Some part of me knew enough to move, though my thoughts were reeling. I lunged for the open door. As soon as I impacted with the bed of the van, Ben gunned the engine and we careened down the street. Emlyn was thrown back against the side of the van. She dropped to her hands and knees, locking eyes with me.

"Hold on!" Ben took the turn at full velocity. The tires squealed against the street beneath us, and I slid further into the van. As we rounded the corner, I caught one last glimpse of Clay and his soldiers through the van's open side door, pounding uselessly down the street after us.

Shaking, I rose to my feet and slid the door shut, locking it for good measure.

Ben risked a look over his shoulder. "Everyone okay back there?"

"Yeah. Yeah." My heart was racing, but my mind couldn't seem to engage.

Emlyn threw herself at me, wrapping her arms around my neck and choking back a sob.

I caught her in my arms and held her. The adrenaline was already fading from my system. My limbs felt leaden, but I clung to Emlyn with a desperate need.

"I love you, too," she whispered into my ear.

"Oh, cricket." The tears I hadn't had time for in close to three days finally breeched their dam.

"That guy...?" Ben glanced at us in the rearview mirror. "That's what you were running from?"

I met Ben's gaze in the mirror, nodding.

"So." He licked his lips, uneasy. "What's the plan?"

"We need to get to New Mexico," I said, surprised to find my voice hoarse and trembling. Emlyn pulled back from me then, her eyes full of questions.

"Great. Okay. New Mexico. That's only about a thousand miles from here, give or take." Ben reached for the radio. "You guys like classic rock?"

"What are you doing?" I slid forward, leaning against the front passenger seat for balance. "You can't drive us to New Mexico. What about your restaurant?"

"That's what managers are for." Ben shrugged. "I'm overdue for a vacation anyway." When I didn't answer, he sighed. "Please. Let me do this for you." Ben gave me a quick glance before turning back to the road.

I studied Ben, uneasy. The mere suggestion that he shouldn't drive us to New Mexico should have stopped him in his tracks…if he'd been enthralled. What if I'd lacked the strength to manipulate him after all? That meant he was doing all this out of the kindness of his heart. I sat back heavily. No part of me felt worthy of his compassion. But then my eyes fell on Emlyn. I might not be worth his kindness, but she was.

"Thank you." I let out a long breath. "I'll find a way to repay you."

"Well," he said, "you could start by telling me your name."

"It's Vyla."

"Okay, Vyla. Why don't you and Em try to get some actual sleep? I know it's not ideal, but there should be an old blanket back there you could spread out on the floor."

Emlyn spotted the blanket and dragged it out. It was some kind of industrial packing blanket, ugly but surprisingly soft. Together we spread the blanket out. It smelled musty, like the earth after a storm. I lay down and Emlyn curled against me, small and warm and *safe*.

I closed my eyes. The swirl of emotions in my mind slowed, losing steam in the face of sleep. Ben navigated us onto the highway, and the van's tires hummed a soothing monotone. Slowly, the tension leached out of my muscles. As I drifted to sleep, one last thought rang in my mind.

Every mile that took us farther away from Clay brought us closer to a better future. Emlyn's future.

About The Author

Originally from New Mexico (and still suffering from Hatch green chile withdrawal), Jenn includes Twentieth Television's *Wicked, Wicked Games* and *American Heiress* among her produced credits. Outside of TV, she created *The Bond Of Saint Marcel* (a vampire comic book mini-series published by Archaia Studios Press), and co-wrote *The Red Star* graphic novels (with creator Christian Gossett from 2007 to 2009). She's also the author of the award-winning *Daughters Of Lilith* YA paranormal thriller novels, and is currently realizing a life-long dream of growing actual real live avocados in her backyard. No guacamole yet—but she lives in hope.

Follow her on Twitter: @jennq
Visit her blog: www.JenniferQuintenz.com

Check out Jenn's *Daughters Of Lilith* novels in print or for your Kindle:
www.amazon.com/Jennifer-Quintenz/e/B0084929JO

"Still Waters"
by Lisa Randolph

I t wasn't even loud enough to wake her. That felt like the most brutally unfair detail of how it all ended. Marion could picture what had happened. Arthur often woke in the middle of the night—a shuffle into the kitchen for a glass of water, a thunderous urination, or what he thought was a secret cigarette smoked just beside the cracked kitchen window. She was a fitful sleeper and forty-six years of marriage had taught her to let these little annoyances go. But the night Arthur fell, resulting in what was undoubtedly an alarming clatter as skull met weathered pine, Marion slept on. When she awoke to find his side of the bed vacant, she thought little of it.

It wasn't until her sleep-filled eyes took in the sight of his crumpled body at the bottom of the stairs that she knew her life was over.

Even two years later the farmer's market presented itself to Rachel as a social gauntlet. How was it possible that in this sleepy little town there was anyone left to wonder, "How is Patrick? Those fish bitin' for him this summer?" And yet she went, for the bulbous tomatoes, for the strawberries still warm from the sun, and most of all for the rhubarb pie crafted by eighty-seven year-old Deirdre Cummings. Rachel had developed a compulsion for well-made desserts since the need to replace the empty hole inside her with refined sugar had made itself so angrily known.

The conversation always went the same: "He passed away ... Yes, cancer ... *Brain* cancer." The mere mention of the tumor that took out New England's beloved son Ted Kennedy was usually enough to shut down even the most prying Vermonter, cancer of course, being the great equalizer. All men fear its unpredictable death knell and the idea that one so young—"Just forty-two! Life can be so unfair..."—could succumb drove them to examine their own mortality, if only for a moment. But two years of questions had a sort of numbing effect on Rachel, and they were often followed with a complimentary potted jam proffered out of guilt. The very mention of cancer now served as a boon to her morning toast.

Rachel took the long way home around the lake, happy to enjoy the ambient scent of fresh apple cider donuts as it wafted from her mesh sack in the Subaru's backseat. But when she saw the sign she stopped the car and pulled over. The Andersons' house was for sale, the bold-lettered eyesore staked into Marion's perfectly manicured lawn. Rachel had heard about Arthur's death. The community of homes surrounding Harvey's Lake was a tiny section of an already tiny town, and an absurdly healthy seventy-year-old man dying after a freak fall down the stairs was the stuff of social headlines.

Marion hadn't been to the farmer's market in months. Rachel had gone through the motions, hoping to repay the many kindnesses friends and neighbors had bestowed upon her years ago: lasagnas and pots of soup were presented with words of sympathy. But Rachel uniquely understood that often quiet, solitude, and body-wracking tears were the only way through to the other side. And though she and Patrick had purchased their own little cabin from the Andersons ten years ago, when the elder couple upgraded to this stately five-bedroom across the lake, the two women had never been friends. Still, Rachel stared at that sign, knowing how much pain hid behind the words "FOR SALE." She reached for the donuts and exited the car, making her way to the front door for an unannounced visit.

Marion assumed it was the realtor. That pesky woman with the ever-present smoker's cough thought nothing of dropping by at any time of day. She needed "unfettered access," she said, though Marion knew it was to make sure the widow hadn't fallen apart, dragging the home's cleanliness down with her. When she opened the door to Rachel Sargeant she was embarrassed to realize her first instinct was to recoil at the possibility of another unidentifiable casserole. The apple cider donuts from Dee Cummings' farmhouse kitchen were something of a relief.

"Would you like some coffee to accompany them?" Marion asked Rachel, insincere.

"Oh, that's all right. They're for you, and I won't stay long," the younger woman said, tossing off her handbag and settling onto a stool at the kitchen island nonetheless.

Marion looked at her, out of practice when it came to small talk, until Rachel blurted it out: "You're selling the house."

"Yes," Marion answered. "I'm told the market hasn't completely recovered, but ..."

"Can I give you some admittedly super unsolicited advice?" Rachel interrupted.

A surprised Marion kept her mouth shut, hoping silence would convey her answer, but Rachel continued. "I thought about listing our cabin, too. Every month we put money aside for that house, even back when I was making four hundred dollars a week as a temp in Manhattan., At the beginning it was just a few bucks in a coffee can, but Patrick said it was the dream that mattered. When he was a famous novelist we'd move up to Vermont, buy a house on a lake with a giant writing desk looking out over the water, and spend our afternoons out on the boat, drinking Negronis and drunkenly making ... " Rachel caught herself, remembering her company, " ... kissing."

Marion listened politely, longing for the moment she could enjoy one of Dee's donuts in peace.

"After he died there was nothing more painful than doing everything we loved to do together without him there. But now ... it's all I have left. It's where I feel him the most, and I just ... I wouldn't want you to miss out on that comfort because it feels impossible right now."

Rachel looked at Marion, indicating that she was finished.

"Is that all?" Marion said.

"Yes. I'm sorry," Rachel answered, sensing the other woman's frostiness, but Marion interrupted. "Then I'll share with you that I don't *want* to sell my house. Not because it concerns you, but because it may put an end to this conversation." Rachel hesitated, having been rebuffed, but it was against her nature to leave a question unanswered. "So then… why?"

Marion looked down, both annoyed and saddened. "Building this house took almost everything we had. Arthur said it was an investment in our future, that we had time to make it back. But now … well, now I'm facing whatever years I have left with a paltry life insurance check in the bank and two children who are in no position to take over my mortgage. This house is all I have. Which means I don't have a choice." Rachel took in the sadness of Marion's situation. "Where will you go?" she said. Marion took a moment to respond, indicating the brown paper sack still on the counter. "Thank you for the donuts."

Even Rachel wasn't bold enough to ignore the hint that their visit was over.

◆ ❖ ◆

"I brought Tito's. Do they even sell vodka out here?" mocked Erin, the giant bottle in her outstretched hand even as she struggled to make her way down the stairs of the monstrous "motor coach," a word that had somehow replaced bus in a pathetic attempt to elevate that almost intolerable mode of transportation. Rachel smiled and helped her friend to the car, eager for both the company and the vodka. Later, they sipped martinis and polished off a platter of local cheeses, the perfect meal in that it required no cooking by the challenged hostess.

"I've come to drag you home with me," Erin said, Rachel stunned by her bluntness. "Hey, we're three martinis in, a best friend knows how to pick her moments."

Rachel jumped up, grabbing more crackers and methodically spreading cheese over one's craggy surface in order to avoid the conversation. "Rach," Erin said. "There's nothing left for you here. All of your friends are in the city, five goddamn hours away. Let us be there for you." Rachel bit into the cracker.

"Cheese. Cheese is here for me, Erin. And it's made less than a mile away by a charming, rotund man named Gus. For real. Gus. That is his name." Erin ignored the attempt at humor.

"I just don't understand how you can stay. Everywhere I look I see Patrick."

"That's exactly why I stay," Rachel answered. "You don't understand."

"You're absolutely right," Erin agreed. "But it's been two years. I need you back. And I think you need us too." Rachel turned her attention to preparing another cracker.

"Marion doesn't understand either. She's selling her house." Erin looked confused. "Marion?" "My neighbor," Rachel explained. "Across the lake. This cabin used to be hers. She and her husband raised their two kids here, then outgrew it. Sold it to us. He just died. Arthur. He just died." Erin watched as her friend tossed another cracker into her mouth.

"That's really sad. But I'm worried about you, not your neighbor."

"I'm okay," Rachel insisted. "I'm dealing with it, I've been dealing with it. And I'm not going to pack up and move back to New York, pretend like I'm ready to start a "new chapter" or some bullshit just to make everyone else comfortable."

There was silence as Rachel left that hanging, suddenly realizing the vodka may have gotten the best of her. "Okay," Erin said. "I'll stop. I want to have fun with you this weekend. And I hope you and Marion are very happy together." Rachel looked up to see a smirk on her face, the tension having passed as it always does with the oldest of friends. Erin had just enough time to dodge the throw pillow tossed at her head.

The sign was still there, but the word "SOLD" written in red negated its original implication. Marion couldn't help looking at it a beat too long every time she walked to the end of the driveway to take in the mail. Today, under the hot sun, the red of those four letters seemed even more final. She saw Rachel walking up the road and briefly considered making a dash for the house until she realized the younger woman had spotted her. She waved brightly and Marion waved back, always the good neighbor. Rachel had a familiar brown paper sack dangling from her hand. "Apple cider donuts. Your favorite," she yelled out, a proclamation that was about as true as one could expect from a woman Marion had so little in common with. Suddenly, Marion's neighborly instincts vanished, and all she could think of was a cup of tea and her book, snuggling under a blanket in Arthur's favorite chair and taking in the smell of him. "I'd ask you in but I'm afraid I'm terribly busy with the move," Marion said, lying easily. "That's okay," Rachel said. "It'll only take a minute. I have a sort of … a proposal for you."

And in that instant, Marion knew exactly what Rachel was going to say.

❖

Rachel had wisely chosen to hire a professional cleaning service. Though she kept a relatively clean house, she had a feeling that her domestic skills were about to be judged like never before. Still, when the doorbell rang she didn't feel ready. There were flowers in charming vases placed in nearly every room, an arrangement of pastries and herbal tea laid out in the kitchen, and one particular guest room, the one Rachel knew had once belonged to Marion's eldest son, was made up with the meticulously embroidered sheets they'd received as a wedding gift from Patrick's grandmother. But the house hadn't truly felt like a home in quite some time, and Rachel hoped her guest wouldn't catch on to what she felt was a pervasive emptiness.

Rachel threw open the door and welcomed Marion with a giant smile, realizing at once how phony she must appear and trying to quash the affected display of enthusiasm. Unsurprisingly, Marion returned the gesture without so much as a smile. She had several pieces of luggage—"only essentials," she'd told Rachel on the phone, having elected to put in storage or sell what her grown children hadn't wanted. "Can I take those for you?" Rachel asked her. "I can manage," Marion answered, carrying the bags up the stairs, and presumably to her room, without any indication of what she felt should be the next step in their cohabitation.

Rachel sunk into one of the kitchen chairs and shoved a croissant into her mouth reflexively. Erin had warned her that she hadn't thought this through, and she was right, of course.. But Rachel couldn't let the lonely woman leave the lake for some awful condominium off the interstate. She knew too well what it took to heal, and this place was a part of Marion's soul, a geographical representation of the history of her family, her marriage. She'd tried to convince herself that Patrick would have wanted it this way, but that was far from the truth. An introvert, Patrick treated the house like a sacred space reserved for writing, entertaining the occasional close friend, and loving on his wife. What was more, he would have been vastly uncomfortable with the implications of the original owner coming home to roost. Rachel had by this time participated in numerous imaginary arguments with her dead husband, each time coming away the victor. "It's just for the rest of the summer," she would say. "Two months, maybe. And then we'll see what happens." Patrick would argue that once the old lady got comfortable, she would stay forever. But Rachel had a tendency to be impulsive.

"May I trouble you for a cup of that tea?" Marion had come downstairs and was looking down at the table spread with goodies, and now, croissant crumbs. "Of course," Rachel said. "That's why it's here," and sprung into action. Marion watched her host, the air between them already charged and awkward. "The room is lovely," she offered. "Daffodils are my favorite flower. So cheerful." Rachel smiled broadly and put the kettle on.

Marion hadn't wanted to make the trip to the market, but she feared Rachel's selection process. From what she'd seen in the weeks thus far, the woman had next to no skills in the kitchen, and a person who does not cook typically lacks the ability to select appropriate food as well. So Marion accompanied her, the first time she'd been since losing Arthur. And she immediately felt the stares.

Rachel had warned her, but Marion brushed it off. She'd lived in this town decades longer, she understood these people. "It's not the people," Rachel had insisted. "They're lovely, and they mean well. But no one knows what to say. So they just ... they *look* at you." Marion wished she had listened. She turned to Rachel and muttered under her breath, "Let's do this quickly, please." Rachel nodded, understanding, and hurriedly paid for the tomatoes and yellow squash she'd already dropped into her bag. Marion made a beeline for Dee's booth, suddenly feeling as though a pie would be the only salve that could help her recover from this now wretched experience. "Hello, Dee," she said. "I'll have a rhubarb if there's one left." Dee smiled at her, making eye contact, which surprised and relieved Marion. "How's Arthur doing? You two go out on the water this morning? It was a beauty, huh?"

Marion immediately regretted turning on her heel and hurrying off. It meant there would be no pie after supper.

Rachel Sargeant was a terribly heavy sleeper. So much so that it had been a problem throughout her life: missed alarms, a complete inability to get out of bed before work to carve out time on the treadmill, and the unlikelihood of nocturnal romps with her beloved husband. But something had woken her, and it was coming from inside the house. It took her a moment to remember that she had a roommate. The month or so Marion had been her guest hadn't been enough for Rachel to grow accustomed to sharing her home again, but it did mean that the likelihood she'd need to use the Louisville Slugger Patrick insisted she keep underneath her side of the bed was slim. She threw off her blankets and made her way down the hall to Marion's room. The door was ajar, and the bed empty. She followed the sound, finding herself at the top of the stairs. There on the landing was Marion, crumpled up in a ball, sobbing quietly. She looked up at Rachel and embarrassment flooded her face. Marion buried her head in her hands, "Go away," she whispered. "Please, please go away." But Rachel ignored her, rushing down the stairs. "Are you hurt? Did you fall?" Marion looked up at her, confused. "Fall?" "Marion, did you hurt yourself?" a panicked Rachel asked again. Marion, finally understanding, shook her head. "I woke up. Thirsty. Got to the top of the stairs and I just ..." As Rachel watched Marion's face twist in agony, she knew what had happened.

It was a very particular kind of post-traumatic stress, the loss of the one most dear to you. In the months following Patrick's death, Rachel's own nights had been torn apart by brutally vivid dreams: Patrick's hospital room, the alarms bleating from the machines on that awful day they finally resigned to performing the tracheotomy, her sweet husband's face contorted in pain even in a drug-induced state approximating sleep. Rachel tried to imagine what Marion felt when she approached the stairs. She pictured Arthur's body, the pain he must have felt as he cracked his head, his final terrified moments alone. No,

Rachel needed no further explanation. "I'm sorry," she whispered. Marion took in the words, finally grateful, and made no effort to avoid Rachel's outstretched arms.

The next morning brought an unseasonable chill, and the lake wore a heavy layer of fog. Marion woke early and brought her much-needed steaming mug of tea down to the water. Her eyes felt near swollen shut. She found one of the kayaks at the edge, the red lightweight single-seater Arthur had always chosen. They'd sold the Sargeants much of the house's accoutrements along with the property itself, secretly overjoyed by the prospect of an upgrade. But her husband was a creature of habit and had never completely taken to the finer equipment. Marion strapped on a life vest, dragged the boat into the water and began to paddle across the lake to the east corner, where it was shallow and tangles of lily pads bobbed along the surface.

She knew it was where the loons built their nest, and soon enough she saw the mother leading her babies out for a swim. Arthur had loved the birds; the singular look of their long black necks and white mottled plumage, and most of all their curious social and breeding patterns that made their study the main event on any freshwater lake in summer. The adults protected their offspring with ferocity and after their hatching, spent summer's end teaching them to swim and fish. Every year, Marion and Arthur followed the little ones' adolescence with great interest, naming them, rating their emerging skills, cooing over their adorable practice of riding around on their mothers' backs.

Arthur's ashes were spread in the lake. When Marion watched a loon dive, she tried to imagine him watching the show from underwater, delighted, at peace.

Rachel returned from her most dreaded of all errands, lugging the bulging reusable shopping bags to the kitchen counter, and was surprised to find the house still empty. Vermont in summer meant there were few necessities one couldn't find at the farmer's market, a nearby honor-system vegetable stand, or one of the many co-ops. But she had a wine habit, and the miserable fluorescent Price Chopper was the grocery store with the best, or perhaps least terrible, selection. Rachel couldn't help but think the worst; Marion was an early riser but it was now mid-afternoon and still no sign of her. Patrick's absence had awakened a fear of the twist of fate, and Marion loved to take morning swims. She finished unpacking the groceries and reached for a sauvignon blanc, the one bottle she'd bothered to buy cold just in case the massive store found her in need of sedation. She poured a glass and carried it to Patrick's writing desk, where her gaze landed on a cribbage board her husband had made during a brief flirtation with woodworking, imagery from their life on the lake whittled into its surface. Rachel could never quite recall the detailed rules of the game, but she did remember countless nights moving the pegs around the board and laughing with friends over glasses of the same nine-dollar bottle of wine from which she'd just poured her own.

Her reverie was interrupted by movement from the sliding glass door, and she looked up to see Marion entering the house with a relaxed smile on her face. "Hi," Rachel said, surprised. "You look … good." Marion crossed to the desk and looked down at the cribbage board. Rachel was still absentmindedly stroking the carving of a loon with her fingertips. "I feel better," Marion said. Rachel knew it best not to press for the source of the older woman's contentment. Marion looked down at the chilled glass of wine. "May I join you?" she wondered. Rachel jumped up to retrieve the bottle.

Marion had been in bed for hours, far from sleep. Rachel had gone out, and it was very late. There was something about the old familiar house that felt quieter than any other spot on the lake, a quality Marion remembered prizing back when her young children fought sleep so valiantly. But as their time together flew by she had grown accustomed to her companion—was that what Rachel was?—and now the emptiness ate away at her. She was relieved to hear the car in the drive, the slamming of the door, until the voices carried up the stairs and into her room. It was a man, unmistakably a man. Hadn't Rachel said she was going for drinks with friends? She never really spoke of friends in town, and until the proclamation of her plans tonight Marion had doubted that she spent time socially with anyone outside New York City. But this man, judging by the way his laugh roared through the house, was quite fond of Rachel. Marion hoped he would leave, having deposited her safely home. Now that Rachel had returned perhaps she could get some sleep. But the sounds of ice clinking in glasses, the turntable springing to life, told her the night was far from over. Marion cursed the thin walls and floors in the old cabin, angry with her former self for pinching pennies when she and Arthur planned the renovation twenty-five years ago. But as the chatter continued she realized she knew the man, recognized the distinct, deep voice as Tom Sullivan, Annie's sweetheart of a son who worked in that charming taproom in Plainfield.

The moment Marion entered the room she knew she'd made a mistake. She tried to turn around, creep back up the stairs unnoticed, but Tom spied her, bellowing, "What the hell?" and climbing off of Rachel, who had opened her shirt for him, baring her bra.

"Marion?" Rachel exclaimed, shocked. "Jesus Christ, Marion, get the fuck out of here!" Rachel's face was red with anger and embarrassment as she rushed to button up. Marion was speechless. "Marion. Please." Rachel repeated, fuming.

Marion looked into her eyes, past the heat of the moment, and for the first time, saw the pity there. "I'm so sorry," Marion said. She climbed the stairs and made her way back into bed, but never could get to sleep.

It had become something of a ritual, these cocktail cruises. Very quickly after she moved in, Rachel learned that Marion hadn't cared much to drink alcohol since her retirement. She explained that with free time stretching out before her, she'd found the need for a more regimented structure to her day, and alcohol only stalled one's productivity. Rachel, of course, felt quite the opposite and had subsequently learned that even an old lady is vulnerable to peer pressure. Today it was gin and tonics, and Rachel knew she'd had one too many. But captaining a pontoon boat required little skill, and the sticky sweet tang of the drink felt as good on her throat as the sun did on her face. In the weeks since Tom had come by for a "nightcap,"

Rachel and Marion had spoken very little. But they still rode beside one another on the boat evening after evening, as much to kill an hour or two as anything.

"You're in too far," Marion scolded her quietly, her eye on the shore. "This spot is less than three feet deep in places."

"I'm aware," Rachel said, sipping her cocktail, and gave the boat a bit more gas. Marion heard the bitterness in her voice. "Are you angry with me, Rachel?"

"Of course not," the younger woman answered, too quickly. Marion pressed her. "If you're not angry, perhaps you're ashamed of your own actions." Rachel almost spit out a mouthful of gin. "And what the hell would make you say that?"

"Watch where you're going," Marion said, alarmed. "The loons nest in this corner."

Not listening, Rachel continued. "Look, I know we're both members of this twisted widow's club and that my cabin—*my* cabin, Marion—is our little clubhouse. But me making out with someone *two years* after Patrick died doesn't mean I loved my husband any less than you loved yours."

"I never said that," Marion answered. "And I don't think that. Now please, focus on the boat." But Rachel couldn't let it go.

"You and Arthur were married for almost fifty years," she said, crumbling. "My husband was diagnosed with a goddamn *brain tumor* at forty-two and died before his next birthday. No one tells you what to do, Marion. They don't tell you how to move on, or if you're even allowed to move on. I'm doing the best I can."

"This is not a contest," Marion answered her, hurt. "I'm an old lady, yes. Arthur was an old man. But your loss isn't bigger than mine, it's not. They're both gone and we're both still here, alone."

Suddenly, Rachel heard a bleating sound, loud and strange and terrible. The loons were screaming. Marion saw that they were nearing the shore and the nest. The mother loon had swum out from the comfort of the brush to signal her defense to the oncoming boat. Marion stood and yanked at the steering wheel, overcoming Rachel's grasp and pointing the boat back toward the center of the lake, away from the birds. A moment passed as she tried to calm herself, knowing any urgency had passed. She then looked down at Rachel. "Get up. I'll steer us home," Marion said, stern. Rachel heard the loon, the cackling cry of distress, begin to fade, and tears started to roll down her face. She moved out from behind the steering wheel and Marion took her seat. They rode home in silence.

♦ ❖ ♦

It was almost surreal, packing to leave her old cabin for the second time. Of course everything looked different, and it was only three suitcases instead of the boxes upon boxes of miscellaneous items that make up a life, but it brought Marion back to a time when she and Arthur had first said goodbye to their days as a young family. The new house had brought with it a new chapter of their life together; they'd even had a tag sale to rid themselves of all Andy and Colin's old toys and baby clothes.

She looked down at the bedside table holding the omnipresent vase of daffodils. Rachel had made sure to replenish them weekly and Marion had enjoyed their yellow aura all summer. She was ready. It was time.

♦ ❖ ♦

"Where exactly is Danvers," Rachel asked, politely. "Is it close to Boston?"

"About a half hour north. Essex County," Colin Anderson answered. "Near the coast."

"Great, that's so great ... It sounds really ... nice," Rachel answered, struggling to further the conversation. Marion's youngest son seemed kind, but the minute she'd heard he was a CPA she knew they would have very little in common. She and Patrick had fought hiring someone to do their own taxes until his first book was published and they realized they actually might be able to buy their lake house, and soon. She guessed that Marion was very proud of her son.

"I want to thank you," Colin said. "This hasn't been easy for any of us, losing Dad. I wanted Mom to move in with us right away, but she wouldn't even consider it. She can be ... particular."

"Try white wine," Rachel said lightly. "It's her weakness." Colin smiled, surprised. He took a moment to consider his next words. "I was against this, her living here. But I think that I, my brother and I ...

we just didn't know what she needed." Rachel smiled back as Marion entered. Colin excused himself and headed upstairs to retrieve his mother's things.

Rachel watched Marion look around the room and could only imagine what she must be thinking. "Will it be okay," she wondered, "Living with them? Will you like it there?" Marion shrugged. "I love my son, but I don't think I'll ever 'like' living anywhere but here, on this lake, with Arthur." Rachel nodded. "But yes," Marion said. "I will be okay. Will you?" Rachel thought carefully before she answered. "I think I will be, yeah. Maybe even soon." Marion looked at her friend, heard her words.

And they understood one another.

About The Author

Lisa Randolph is a television writer with a diverse group of drama credits that include *Being Human*, *The Shield*, and *Gilmore Girls*. Lisa hails from Canton, Connecticut and graduated with a Bachelor of Music in Voice from New York University.

Follow her on Twitter: @LisaMRandolph

"Martyoshka"
by Kay Reindl

Ava pictured the Brown acceptance packet sitting on the polished mahogany table with the rest of the mail. She could see its brown corner barely visible. She knew what it would look like. Feel like. Because she'd gotten four other acceptance packets already.

Her life was right around the corner, and that corner was a good college. It had to be. She'd waited long enough for her life to start. She knew how lucky she was to have such a promising life, but there was always something hidden in the darkness of her history that whispered to her that it wasn't luck. It was something else. And she would have to pay for it. She never knew what to do with this awful voice, so she did her best to ignore it.

Her dad's car was there when she got home. He'd come home sick again. Her dad was sick a lot, but there was nothing wrong with him. He just had one of those sensitive immune systems, the doctors said. Her dad told Ava not to worry. A day in bed and he'd be at it the next day. Everything would work out, because he made things happen. He'd made this life happen. How could she not believe him?

There was mail for her but it wasn't from Brown. It was a small box wrapped in brown paper. Her name was carefully printed in blocky black ink. The return address didn't look familiar, and there was no name. Five faded stamps were lined up perfectly, as if given up with great care. She carefully tore the stamps from the package as she opened it. Inside crackly white tissue paper was a wooden nesting doll. A happy smiling old woman in a dress and apron, painted in formerly bright but now faded primary colors. Ava gently twisted it open, but there was nothing inside. The doll had that long-ago tang of old wood.

161

She put the doll back together again and held it up to the light. Where the doll twisted apart, the paint was chipped. All over her shiny round body, paint was rubbed off, as if she'd been played with. Loved.

Ava crept upstairs with the package and the doll. She dumped her books on her desk and set the doll on her dresser, next to the willowy ballerina statue and other things that had been curated by her dad's former girlfriend. Jaime would have said that the cheap wooden doll threw off the balance of the room, which is what she said about the plastic horse Ava had won at the fair before throwing it in the trash.

She stared at the doll for a long moment. She could see it on another shelf, among other heirlooms. It didn't fit in Ava's blue and green room, with its exotic silk duvet and hundred-dollar pillows. Ava had been appropriately enthusiastic when Jaime had revealed the design to her, but it wasn't really Ava's. The doll didn't fit the room, but it fit Ava. She didn't know why, or how. She reached for the packaging, smoothing out the stiff brown paper. She looked up the return address on her phone. It was in the old city, which had become an echoing old ghost when the businesses decided to abandon it and make something new.

Ava could drive her new car to the address, to find out who'd given this to her. Her hands tingled with excitement. She was going to do this. And she didn't want to wait until tomorrow after school. It was still early. She'd blow off Prom Committee and look into her mystery.

Even from far away, I could tell how perfect she was. She had that aura about her that said she'd been chosen. She had everything she could ever want. I swallowed my hatred for her and forced myself to focus. I wanted more than anything to put a bullet through her brain. Or to wrap my hands around her neck and watch her privileged life leak away as I choked her. But she was the first. I had to wait.

Ava watched her home grow smaller as she drove across the vast bridge that connected the city to its predecessor. Leaving the bridge, the smoothly paved highway gave way to a rough, pitted road. There

162

were no streetlights. No street signs. This was the old city, settled almost a century ago by hard-working, honest people who had built it into a thriving town big enough for the modern conveniences but still small enough for people to know their neighbors.

But the town grew just plentiful enough for the company to see value in it. They moved in and ripped the heart out of the city. They built the bridge, and the chosen ones moved away to the new city Ava lived in. The old city was a violent place now. The people who stayed, who tried to help, were destroyed. The others became savage in order to survive there. People fought for it, for a while. But there was no victory to be won. Just a bad place to be abandoned.

Ava drove down a main street pitted with potholes and lined by broken, abandoned storefronts. But as she crawled to a stop at a dented stop sign, Ava could see life in those storefronts. There were businesses, protected by iron grates, but they were open. Selling cut-rate clothing and electronics to shifty-eyed men and women. Ava was struck by how young everybody was. They'd been raised in this city. They knew nothing else. She felt sorry for them.

◆ ❖ ◆

I followed her from the rooftops. Nobody looked at me anymore. They were used to me. They kept their eyes on the street, not getting involved. They couldn't. They'd be hurt, or worse. They knew that by now. But they didn't know how much I cared for them. They didn't believe anybody could.

◆ ❖ ◆

Ava turned off the main street into a residential area of dilapidated houses and rickety apartment buildings unhappily crowded together. A dog barked, and Ava glanced over to see a boy in a hoodie walking a fat little puppy. The boy was hunched over, hands in his pockets, eyes scanning the cracked sidewalk. He straightened up when Ava passed, his eyes on the shiny new car that she had been stupid enough to drive here. She checked her phone service. Luckily, she had a few bars. She wondered if there were even police in this apocalyptic place.

Her destination, a small clapboard house, was on the right. The paint was so faded and peeling that it was hard to tell what color the house had been. Ava parked and looked around for a long moment. The boy with the dog had gone. The street was quiet. She got out, making sure to lock the car, and walked up to the house. The windows were dark, the curtains semi-drawn. Mail was piled up on the porch. She kicked the pile with her foot, revealing fliers for swap meets. Wrestling matches. Raves. Strip clubs. Every activity in this town was one of desperation. Ava rang the cracked plastic doorbell, but it made no sound. So she knocked. Timidly, at first. Then harder.

The door pushed open. It was probably the only house in the old city that wasn't locked up tight. The front room was dark and smelled musty and forgotten. Whatever life this house had had before had left it. A dingy, formerly green sofa sagged against the far wall. Before it, a scratched wooden coffee table sat on a stained, threadbare rug. And, on the mantel, a nesting doll.

Ava went in, footsteps making the brittle floorboards creak. She picked up the doll. It was a size smaller than the one she had been sent. A younger woman. Still smiling. Rosier cheeks. Blond hair under a white cap.

An image came to her: Three more dolls, lined up on a wooden shelf. Before she knew what she was doing, Ava turned down the short hallway toward the room at the end of the hall.

I watched her through the windows as she went into the room that had been hers as a child. She went to the shelf with the last two dolls. I had the final doll. I put my hand in my pocket and felt for it. Rolled it between my fingers. Wondered if I'd get to use it.

The dolls fit in this room. Ava had memories of being here. Living here. They hadn't been able to afford toys when she was younger. She'd made worlds out of paper and her father's pens. Houses and streets and people. She'd invented vacations for her lucky people. During the summer they went to a lake with cabins, canoes, and picnics. For the holidays, they went to a city that wasn't unlike the city she lived in now. She'd heard a song about frosted windowpanes that brought to mind a Christmas where snow fell and store windows were decorated and cheerful packages were tied up with string. She would look out the window as the slanting rain fell from the mud-splashed sky and smile, because she believed in her fantasy Christmas.

Her parents fought then. She'd shut her door and make her fantasy world as they yelled at each other. She didn't hear any words because she didn't want to. But one night, her father had come in and told her that their luck had changed. They were leaving and going someplace wonderful. She would never have to see this place again.

She didn't know what luck was, so he'd explained it to her. Luck was something that special people were given because they deserved it. He led her past her mother's door, which was shut. She wanted to know why her mother wasn't coming with them, but she never asked because luck and fortune sounded like the embodiment of everything she fantasized. Maybe Mom would come later.

But she never did. Later, her father told her that her mother didn't want to be a part of their family anymore. Ava never asked about her.

She didn't hear me come in, because I didn't want her to. She sat on the floor, probably like she'd done as a kid, and I could tell by the way her shoulders slumped that she remembered that this had been her house. I wanted to take out the knife and slit her throat. But I'd learned lessons, too.

"Turn around." My voice was hoarse. Gritty with anger.

She jumped to her feet with a lot more grace than I thought she had and whirled around, holding her cellphone like it was a weapon.

"I'm not going to hurt you," I told her. Her face was white. The edges that had been smoothed away after she'd left this house were back. She looked like she belonged here again.

"Did you send me here?" she asked.

"Yeah, I did. You need to know the truth."

"The truth about what?"

She knew damned well what, so I just stared at her, cold-eyed.

"What happened? Why am I here?"

Oh, I'll tell you what happened, rich girl. Your father ruined my life so that he could get ahead. He destroyed his own marriage, too, and then he took you away and gave you everything you ever wanted. He numbed you to the truth, but you know what happened. You know exactly.

I didn't say any of that. I took out the plastic bag. Opened it. Carefully removed the newspaper clipping, which had started to brown because that had been awhile ago. I carried it everywhere with me because when I'd seen it, I'd found out who my father was.

She could tell that it meant something to me.

"Who are you?" Her voice was softer. She wasn't afraid anymore.

So I handed her the piece of paper that had changed both of our lives.

Ava was nearly certain that the violent-looking girl wasn't going to hurt her. She took the newspaper clipping and made a show of handling it carefully, which seemed to relax the girl. It was an old story, from twelve years ago. There had been an explosion at a warehouse that had finally, irrevocably, torn out the heart of the old town.

The company that had owned the warehouse, the last bastion of hope in the old city, went under. The lives of the people who depended upon the warehouse were destroyed. When Ava saw the old company's logo, she recognized it. She'd seen it every day, on her father's uniform. He'd worked there. He protected it. But he hadn't protected it that night.

Amazingly enough, there had been only one fatality. A man named Nathan Chambers, who had saved eight peoples' lives but had given his own.

Nathan Chambers had been survived by his ten-year-old daughter, Lucy. Ava looked up from the story into the eyes of Lucy Chambers.

Ava's father was supposed to protect the building, and Lucy's father had died. That's why Ava had been brought here. To know the truth.

I could tell by the look of sympathy that flashed across her face that she thought she understood. But she didn't know. I needed her to see the horror. To feel what I'd felt for the past twelve years.

"My father protected this city," I said. "He was born here. It was a nice place then. But corruption came, and he fought against it. He had to keep that identity a secret because he was a threat to the corporation. They wanted to kill him, but they didn't know who he was. So they lured him to the warehouse. All they needed was to make the security guard look the other way while they set the charges, before my father entered the building. And they paid well for it."

Oh, yes. Now she saw.

◆ ❖ ◆

Ava heard the words now. The fight between her parents. Her mother kept asking why, in increasingly rising tones. They didn't need the money. Her father wouldn't listen. They could leave this place now. Start over. But her mother wouldn't leave. This was her home. She gave Ava's father an ultimatum, so he took Ava and left.

"My mother didn't want to come with us," Ava said. "My dad said she refused to come."

Lucy sighed. Impatient. "He took you in the middle of the night. He didn't even tell her he was going. Your mother tried to find you, but she couldn't. She stayed here because this was your home. She hoped you'd come back someday. She stayed here, and she died here."

Ava sank to the floor as Lucy told her how the violence had gotten out of control when the criminals learned that the city's protector was dead. They'd tried to steal her mother's meager possessions. She'd fought back, and died for it.

"It was about a year later," Lucy said.

A year after they'd moved. When her father had met Jaime, and Ava had gotten her brand-new bedroom set. The bile rose in her throat as she remembered her mother's face, that kind, honest person who did the best she could. And her father, the man who had justified what he'd done. But he'd saved Ava, hadn't he?

"He loves me," Ava said. "He loved me so much that he gave up everything to take me away from this."

Lucy laughed, and Ava froze. Those were the words her father had used, when she'd cried for her mother and her home. He told her how much he loved her, and how much better her life was now. Eventually she'd given in. Accepted it.

"I made myself forget," she said.

"No kidding," said Lucy. "How nice it must be, to have everything you want. I only want one thing. Revenge."

A chill went down Ava's spine. That's why she was here. Lucy was going to take her away from her father. Lucy was going to kill her.

"I don't care," Ava said dully. "If you're going to, just do it."

"Oh, honey. I don't want revenge against you. I wanted you to know what your daddy did. Next move is yours."

Ava thought about her life, about what she was waiting for. About how she'd never see her mother again. About how her dad's one action had destroyed so much.

"I'll talk to him. To my dad," she said. "I'll get him to tell me the truth."

"I already told you the truth," Lucy said. "What good will that do?"

"Then what do you want from me?" Ava asked.

"I told you. The next move is yours. Don't wait for me to tell you."

Ava always did what her teachers told her to do. She did the extra credit. She had the right friends. Bought the right things. Laughed the right way. This was too different for her to contemplate.

"I'm going to talk to him," she said.

Lucy glared at her, and then walked away without a word.

Ava took the other nesting dolls with her. She went home. Had some dinner. Waited for her dad to come home. When he did, he poured himself a glass of Scotch and sat down with a sigh. He smiled at her, but the smile didn't reach his eyes. She realized that it never did. He got his phone out and looked over his schedule. He was an executive with the corporation, and now she knew how he'd gotten that job. He wore a nice suit every day and was always tired. He never talked about it. They never talked about anything.

But things were different now. She put one of the nesting dolls on the polished counter in front of him. He glanced at it.

"What's this?"

"Mom's, I think," Ava said. "From the old house."

He got very still and turned his phone over, setting it down with a click.

"What were you doing there?" he asked. Then he coughed, a hacking wheeze that doubled him over. He'd been sick since they moved here. And now Ava knew why. He was being poisoned by what he'd done. By the sacrifice he'd talked himself into making for his daughter, when it was just selfish. It had destroyed the old city. It had gotten Ava's mother killed.

As he coughed, Ava thought about how happy Lucy must have been as a girl, until her father was taken from her. Identified as a hero. Mourned for the sacrifice that didn't matter because the corporation got what it wanted. And Ava's dad had helped them.

His eyes widened. She felt a weight in her hand and realized she'd picked up a knife. She looked at her distorted image in the shiny blade. She wanted to plunge it into his stomach. To release the poison that was inside him. Would that release hers, too? As she turned the knife over, things became clear. She'd seen her father talking to hard-looking men. She'd heard them discuss deals, both financial and violent. Her father had been rewarded with a seat at the table. Their money was tied up in all of this. Her money. For college. To start her life.

That's why she always looked to the future, because, unconsciously, she was trying to escape what her father had done. And now she'd seen the sadness of the old city. The people who swam against the tide every day, who were denied better lives because rich men wanted to get richer.

Ava was only one person. One spoiled teenage girl. She couldn't do much, but she could do this. She could rid the city of one cancer.

Her father stood, seeing the look set in her eyes. "Ava. What are you doing?"

"Mom died," Ava said, her voice cracking against her will. "She died because you were greedy."

"Your mother died because she was selfish," her father said, using his tactic of reflecting his own weaknesses back onto innocent people. "I've given you everything. All you could want. You can go to any school you want to, because of me."

"I don't want to go," she said.

169

"Don't be ridiculous. Of course you do. It's our dream." Her father used the dismissive voice that he'd had to use a lot when they first came here. Before the psychiatrists had worked their magic to convince Ava that her "before" life didn't matter, and didn't define her. Before he'd started to manipulate her so she'd fall in line. She wanted to kill him. She wanted to see his blood pool on the polished floors. She wanted vengeance. But while it would make her feel good for a moment, it wouldn't bring her mother back. It wouldn't fix what he'd done.

"You didn't give me my dreams. You gave me yours," she said. "How many lives did you ruin? You've already destroyed one city. You'll kill this one, too. You and your business partners. And then what? Will you find someone weak like you who will do your dirty work? Will you just keep doing it? Over and over again?"

She stepped forward.

"I'm going to stop you," she said.

He laughed, and she could see how cruel he was. How inhuman.

"You're going to do what, Ava? You're a kid. And you have no proof. I should have left you there with your mother. You don't deserve the life I've given you."

It was an empty threat, because Ava knew she wasn't going to take his money. She wouldn't go to college and cocoon herself against her father's treachery.

"I'm going to make sure that you lose everything," she said, her voice steadier than it had ever been.

"You can't do anything to me," he spat at her. "You're powerless. Get out of my house."

"Technically, you can't throw me out until I'm eighteen, but I guess you could just work something out with one of your evil lawyers," she said, surprised by her quick comeback. "But don't worry, Daddy. I'm going."

She put the knife down on the counter and walked away.

I found her in the old house. I hoped she'd come back, preferably not covered in her father's blood. And she wasn't. She hadn't killed him.

She looked up when I came in and I could tell she'd been crying. She needed to, and she knew it.

"I almost threw a knife at him," she said in a voice stuffed with tears.

"You don't know how to handle a knife," I said. "That would have been embarrassing. You'd totally miss."

A faint smile out of her.

"Where's the doll?" she asked.

"What doll?"

"The last one. The center."

I took the small wooden doll out of my pocket and handed it to her. She turned it over in her hand. It looked like her: Brown hair. Blue eyes. Solemn. Knowing.

"It's just the MacGuffin, isn't it? My mom never had these dolls."

I didn't know what that meant, but she was right. I nodded.

"How did you make me think they were hers?"

I shrugged. "Everyone has something like this in their past. It's a symbol. Like peeling back an onion until you get to the heart."

I knew onions didn't have hearts, but she nodded because she got it.

"You wanted me to see the truth," she said.

She held the little doll up to eye level. "So this is me now. The center. No more layers. Nothing else to explore."

"I think now you add your own layers," I said.

She looked from the doll to me. "You're going to save the city, aren't you?"

"I'm going to try," I said.

"And then what?"

"Then what?" I asked. "You don't think that's enough?"

"I think you want to bring them down, so they can't do this again. It can't just be revenge. You have to get something else out of it," she said, like she knew.

And she did, I guess. So I told her to come with me. "I'm taking you to my lair."

She grinned. She was starting to get me.

◆ ❖ ◆

Lucy's lair was in the basement under her crumbling house, which had been nice once. It was stocked with computer equipment. A gym. All the stuff Lucy had been using for years, as she went after the criminals in the city and learned about the men in the corporation.

In the corner was a stack of brown boxes. Inside were dozens of sets of nesting dolls. She didn't have to say anything to me. I knew what we were going to do.

We were going to make people remember.

About The Author

Kay Reindl is an actual native Californian whose first job in television was as a staff writer on the Fox TV series *Millenium*. Since then, she's written for numerous series including *Moonlight* and *Twisted* and the animated series *Scooby-Doo Mystery Incorporated* and *Beware The Batman*. She's sold TV pilots and has self-published two novels on Amazon, because why not? She is on a never-ending quest for the perfect conspiracy theory. To this day, her family still has no idea what she does every day.

Follow her on Twitter: @KayReindl
Read her blog: www.seriocity.blogspot.com

"Bat Girl"
by Kira Snyder

Hildy had long, thick hair of a rich red color, keen blue eyes, and skin that was pale and flawless. These were her best features, the ones people noted first to avoid mentioning that she was a woman of some size. Not enough to cause comment in most places, but Hildy lived in Los Angeles, a city that she secretly suspected of having body-fat monitors at the airport and bus stations and highway mountain passes, used to help weed out the zaftig before they entered the city limits.

Hildy had a broad, pleasant face. She rarely smiled with her teeth showing; people assumed she had braces. Her name was short for Hildegard and was the same as a fast-talking, glamorous character from an old movie Hildy liked. Hildy herself was not, generally speaking, good with words, nor glamorous. She looked about 30.

She was not an actor. She was a lighting technician, in film and theater. Every day she wore a clean black T-shirt with black jeans and black sneakers, the better to move around in the wings without being seen. Her glorious hair usually was twisted up in a bun with a pencil. Around her waist she wore a belt that held a flashlight, wrench, utility knife, tape, and cell phone in individual holsters. In this respect she looked no different from the other technicians, but thanks to the belt and the color of her hair, which was similar to that of an actress in an old superhero TV show, Hildy had acquired the occasional nickname Bat Girl.

Despite her size, in the dark Hildy moved like a cat, never misstepping among the tangles of cable and rigging, able to climb nimbly up ladders and vanish into the shadows high above the stage floor.

She was very good at her job. Lighting designers and cinematographers never failed to be impressed at her evanescent creations of light and shadow. Homely actors, their plainness usually hidden from the public by phalanxes of stylists, bloomed under the lights she focused on them.

Hildy herself was particularly proud of how she was able to duplicate the warm, buttery sunlight of a summer morning, about 10 a.m. in the mountains.

Because of her skill, Hildy had her pick of jobs, and chose ones that shot at night or only on interior sets. She felt awkward and bulky unless indoors, in the dark, her pale skin going wan under the unrelenting Southern California sun. If anyone cared to look, she appeared almost ill in the daylight, as if it hurt her.

The women who called themselves Hildy's friends saw her as a project.

"Sweetie, this is not helping," they scolded through mouthfuls of corn chips that they would find in Hildy's cupboards.

"Bat Girl, you have to remove temptation," they counseled while licking chocolate frosting from the cupcakes she kept in an airtight plastic box on the countertop.

They didn't seem to notice that Hildy herself never seemed to eat anything, although her kitchen was always full of the things they routinely denied themselves and secretly craved.

Glossy photographs of classic movie stars covered all the mirrors in Hildy's home. For motivation, her friends reasoned. After all, didn't Marlene Dietrich have her back teeth removed to make her face thinner?

Hildy lived in an apartment in a lovely old mission-style building dating from the 1920s. There were high ceilings and hardwood floors, and the building was home to at least two famous scandals of Hollywood's Golden Age.

The neighborhood could charitably be described as colorful, but Hildy's block was peaceful and safe. Drug dealers had once moved into a shabby old house across the street to set up a methamphetamine lab. A string of break-ins started on the streets around Hildy's, and two drive-bys sprayed the neighborhood with freely careening bullets. Terrified of the lean, angry men who lived in the house, no one reported anything.

One day, the trouble stopped. Some time later the police showed up to the house in response to a smell reported by the mailman.

Inside, the dealers were all quite dead, pale where rot had not yet set in. They apparently had turned on one another, the floor glittering with fragments of shattered mirror. Their throats had been torn out. There was very little blood.

The coroner's assistants had seen worse. A bad batch of meth, they reasoned, plus possibly animal predation. Coyotes, maybe.

"How horrible!" Hildy's friends chirped over sugary sodas from Hildy's fridge. "I bet that happens a lot around here," they added hopefully. Hildy assured them that it did not. They seemed disappointed when further grisly acts failed to materialize outside Hildy's charming mullioned windows.

Hildy's friends believed such an apartment was wasted on Hildy and her ever-changing collection of tropical fish. She had no boyfriend that anyone could recall, nor a girlfriend for that matter.

Upstairs lived Anthony, a costume designer, who was sick. He had over fifty pills that he had to take every day, and occasionally was too weak to work, but Anthony was one of the lucky ones. Many of the men and boys he knew had already died from the same disease poisoning his blood.

Anthony pulled no punches, having decided that life was too short to be polite. "Those bitches will suck you dry," he said with a sigh to Hildy, passing her friends on the front steps as they were leaving, their hands still sticky with cinnamon crumbs.

But Hildy had long ago learned to take friendship where she could. Sometimes she'd sit on her patio ("Look at the size of this patio! Think of the parties you could throw here!" her friends would lament to one another) and sing songs to herself, quietly, but not quietly enough not to be heard by Anthony upstairs, sketching with his colored pencils at a drafting table by his open French doors.

The songs were sweet, and sad, in a language he didn't recognize, but his mind called up images of mountains far away—sharp, craggy, hard mountains, with jewellike valleys of villages between, lights sparkling against the night. Anthony would shiver, but not be able to stop listening.

He could always tell the sketches he drew while Hildy sang. Those were the designs the directors raved about, that the costumers did their best work on, that actors did their best work in. "They're just so right," Anthony's thrilled clients would say with a smile. "So true to the story. To the vision. So true." One design, a delicate wedding dress sketched as Hildy hummed a rare cheerful melody (one fish had just given birth), had helped win Anthony an award.

Hildy's current job was on a new TV show, one that aspired to be hip and funny and that featured a young, beautiful cast. In this respect it was no different from a dozen or so other shows on the air, but this was the newest entry and so had an air of freshness reflected in the reviews and ratings. The producers were giddy with praise, and a lavish Halloween party up in the Hollywood Hills was scheduled.

Three of Hildy's friends were in the cast. The girls were thin and tan and enjoyed gossiping to Hildy. They lived in constant hope that she would reciprocate, knowing that she, like most crew members, had access to some of the best dirt there was. But Hildy would just smile, lips closed, and shake her head.

The day before the party arrived, and Hildy revealed to the trio that she had no plans to go.

"But you have to! We have a great idea for a group costume!" the blondest one said. The three girls always spoke as a unit.

"It's kind of a superhero thing. It's a theme!" the strawberry-blonde said.

"We think it'll be cool, Bat Girl. Comic books are retro-hip right now," said the brown-blonde one, who due to her hair color felt pressure to be more serious and intellectual than her companions.

"We'll send it over tomorrow. You'll look fabulous," the blondest one said.

They were not particularly talented actresses, and Hildy did not miss the smirky little smile they exchanged. Hildy was not stupid.

Halloween made Anthony sad. Most holidays did; he missed his lover. Lonely in the gathering dark, he pounded on Hildy's door, a jack-o'-lantern in hand. He nearly dropped it when Hildy opened the door.

"Those bitches," Anthony whispered.

Hildy stood before him, squeezed miserably into a caped outfit of purple spandex, the shoddy material unforgiving, cinching her ample body into rolls and bumps. A belt strained around Hildy's waist, a bat embossed on the cheap plastic buckle. A mask with tiny bat ears covered her face and gorgeous hair.

"Those. Skunk-mean. *Cunts.*" No longer a whisper.

It didn't matter, Hildy told him. She wasn't going.

"Not in that, you're not," Anthony fumed, and seized her by the hand.

Hildy had never been inside Anthony's apartment before. She didn't like going to other people's homes and seeing the small, mundane objects of their lives. Their shoes, spoons, framed pictures of the dead. How precious and ordinary and fragile, she would think, sorrowful. People never remember that in time they will be a dead face in someone else's frame.

But Anthony knew this about himself and didn't care that his home was full of pills and too many such framed pictures. It was also full of Mardi Gras beads, African drums, fresh fragrant roses, movie posters, and overstuffed brocade furniture that looked like it too had been in movies. Hildy liked Anthony's apartment.

Anthony fussed at a dressmaker's dummy, then stood back. "It's for a new opera. It's for the Vampire Queen."

The gown was deepest blue silk, almost black, the sleeves scalloped like wings and intricately embroidered in silver, alight with jewels that Hildy knew were plastic but that caught the light like the diamonds they were supposed to be. It was the most beautiful thing Hildy had seen in a very long time.

"It'll look fantastic with your hair. Try it on."

Hildy had seen enough movies to know what Vampire Queens were supposed to look like. They were slender and dark-haired. Poised. Delicate.

"Bullshit," growled Anthony. "Vampires are from Central fucking Europe. Have you ever seen women from Central Europe?"

Hildy had.

The dress fit ("Of course it fits! How many size two sopranos do you know?"). Hildy stroked the fabric of the skirt as Anthony brushed her hair until it gleamed.

"You're a vision," Anthony said, simply. "See?" He flung open the closet door, behind which was a full-length mirror. Startled and alarmed, Hildy said something then, sharply, but he didn't understand the words.

That was the last thing Anthony remembered before awakening on his couch, the doorbell ringing. A goblin in search of candy. Hildy was gone.

Hildy's friends from the TV show were at the DJ-loud, mobbed party already. One girl was dressed as a cat in tight leather, another in a star-spangled corset, the third in a blue teddy with red boots and a little red cape. They were annoyed, drunk with male attention and pink vodka. Hildy was late. "We're supposed to come as a *group*; that's the whole *point* of a group costume," they whined to the disinterested bulk of the hired security guard.

Hildy found them inside the mansion's vaulted main room, or rather they found her, turning in confusion at the awed murmurs and parting crowd.

Hildy strode in, regal, head high, wearing the exquisite gown as if clothed in the night sky itself. Her hair cascaded down her back like flames. She was magnificent, suddenly the only woman in the room.

"Hildy?" one of her friends ventured.

Hildy raised her arms, the winged sleeves unfolding, and began to sing. And as she sang, she smiled.

Hildy, her friends learned, did not wear braces.

Later, the police had no idea what to make of the reports. People talked of seeing monsters. Actresses who knew they were lovely appeared pocked and diseased to their companions. Men who lived extravagant lifestyles, denying themselves nothing, saw themselves in the mansion's leaded mirrors as grasping, clawed beasts, dressed in tattered and rotted finery. Darker animals were uncloaked, the addicts and criminals and child pornographers, suddenly appearing as their true selves.

In the panic and madness, fights erupted; windows were broken. No one was quite sure just when the house caught fire.

It seemed insane to the police that someone could be *singing* in the midst of all this, but that was the one thing all the reports had in common, although no one could recall who it was. The police chalked the whole mess up to bad acid and set about calling lawyers, rehab centers, and, with not a little pleasure, the press.

"So bombed they couldn't even remember if it was a woman or a man singing," one police officer chuckled to another as she dialed.

Hildy walked down the front steps of the mansion, leaving it burning behind her in the night, crazed party guests fleeing the fire or their onetime friends or themselves. She flicked some ash off her skirt that had settled there from a smoking upper floor.

She realized she wasn't singing alone. Another voice had joined hers, a man's. He knew the words, the old words. He was tall and broad, some would say heavyset. His face was pleasant but unremarkable. He was the security guard. He looked like he was from Central Europe.

They regarded each other with surprise and recognition.

His name was Walt, short for Walter, a character from an old movie Walt liked, a man who was suave and handsome, although Walt knew he was neither. Like Hildy, Walt wasn't an actor. He was a bouncer. He worked at night.

Hildy's friends don't come around much anymore. Hildy doesn't mind; she has a new roommate and a new double-size fish tank.

While the apartment building's management company initially frowned at these changes, a note from the landlord quieted them. If anyone cared to look, the handwriting of the note is the same as the signature on the original lease from eighty years ago, and both curiously similar to Hildy's own.

Sometimes she and Walt sit in the shade of their patio, the windows open, and sing quietly together, songs she had forgotten she knew.

Anthony's mantel groans with awards.

About The Author

Kira Snyder has written for TV shows *The 100* on the CW, *Incursion* for Starz, Syfy's *Eureka* and *Alphas*, and the CBS vampire cult hit *Moonlight*. The *Parish Mail* ebooks, Kira's interactive Young Adult mystery series, are available now on many digital platforms. Also a game designer, Kira has created games for Microsoft, the MIT Press textbook *Rules Of Play*, and Electronic Arts, including the seminal alternate reality game *Majestic*. Kira is a proud geek and loves both science and sci fi, reading when she's not writing.

Follow on Twitter: @sugarjonze

Check out Kira's *Parish Mail* ebooks here:
www.coliloquy.com/productscat/parish-mail

"Crystal Brook"
by Jeane Wong

The blue shutters and white paneling of this sprawling mansion hadn't aged a day.

Everything about the home was suspended in time, like little critters embedded in amber. The houses on Mill Lane in Stamford, Connecticut were always enchanting, despite their gothic facades. It was the way the afternoon light hit the angles of the pointed windows and arches of these homes. The light resembled little yellow particles doing pirouettes in the air. And not to discount the beauty she saw here, she felt it was the people who used to be here that made this a magical place. The only jarring feature of the mansion was on the front lawn, where the foreclosure sign laid on its side. The new owners probably haven't had a chance to get rid of the sign yet, she thought.

With the sleeve of her shirt, she pushed her bangs out of her eyes but forgot she shaved her hair off. Old habits, you know, die hard. Instead, she wiped away a bead of sweat. She crept in slowly, trying to keep her bulky backpack from making too much noise. She wasn't scared. She had been through worse. So undaunted by the idea of trespassing, one bald girl crouched and looked in every direction ten times. She tripped over the same rock twice. Some people make the worst criminals.

She unhinged a window panel on the first floor that led to an inner garden, a trick she learned when she used to sneak boys in growing up. She walked through the inner garden, now a dusty path with weeds and a bevy of flattened moving boxes. The house was put on the market almost a year ago when they found out about the cancer. The money from the sale of the house came through a month ago, but it was already too late. Sure, you can pay old medical bills off but not new treatment if the person's already dead.

Pushing aside her sudden anger, she saw the new owners had pulled out the flowers and poured in concrete, which covered some of the path. She could already tell the owners had no sense of taste. Now she was annoyed. Even with money, they lacked the ability to create even an adequate home. Instead, some people get rid of the old. She had an involuntary jerk thinking about this, but soon it wouldn't matter. She arrived at Crystal Brook. The sunlight made a halo around her silhouette.

Before her was a flowing stream, wild grass surrounding the water and scattered volcanic rocks all around, all leading to a mini-castle on a distant hill. This is how the two kids rendered this dream-like place growing up. Crystal Brook was like Shangri-La, Narnia, or Terabithia: a place in one's imagination. But in real life, Crystal Brook was actually a tree house built in the backyard of 1249 Mill Lane that connected to the inner garden and it was a place named after two best friends—Crystal and Brook.

Simply put, yes, Crystal Brook was a tree house. But in the eyes of these kids, it was a castle on a hill. And the puddle inside the tree house from the leaky roof was a large pond, where these two friends would skip stones, for hours on end. One time Crystal hung a mirror inside, and the mirror shifted to become a hall of mirrors, where the kids made silly faces, which reflected in patterns all along the walls. A chocolate bar turned into a treasure chest that overflowed with gummy bears, lollipops, and more chocolate treats.

Crystal was five years old when she met Brook. He was the son of the housekeeper who lived with her family. Not being very remarkable, he was a chubby boy and a shy kid with jet-black hair, brown skin, and light eyes that were green or blue depending on the shirt he wore. He spent most of his time hiding behind his mother and speaking in faint whispers of Spanish. The first words he uttered in front of Crystal were, "*Estoy asustado*." I'm scared. He was a peculiar young boy. But Crystal soon learned he was more than a quiet weird boy, because he had a mind that could make the impossible a reality.

Crystal was the Snow White version of Brook, with fair skin that burned far too easily, and matte black hair and blue eyes; she was a pint-sized doll. Socially, she didn't understand the girls her age, who wanted to drink tea from empty cups, or the boys, who liked burning ants on the sidewalk. Brook was welcome refreshment. Growing up as an only child, Crystal was excited to have a friend. Brook's mother was happy to have Brook practice his English and come out of his shell.

At the bottom of the tree, Crystal traced her fingers over a handmade wooden sign: *"Crystal Brook—Beware!"* She peered up at the tree house and its small opening. Could she fit in the doorway? She ballooned three dress sizes this year from the stress of everything. When she turned 37 a few months ago, her body refused to acknowledge the concept of dieting and weight loss. The process of putting on clothes had been like waddling around like a blind bear, with her top always stuck midway over her head, or hopping about like a kangaroo, trying to fit into her favorite not-so-skinny jeans. Not minding the present challenge, Crystal climbed up the tree and sucked in her belly. She pushed aside some old cobwebs and squeezed her way in, like forcing the last dollop of ketchup out of a bottle.

She opened her backpack, taking out an urn and various photos of her and Brook. One photo was of them as kids pointing to the sign in the tree house, and another image was one with their faces painted at a college football game. There was a span of a few years when they never saw each other. They went to separate high schools. And the last photo was of Brook and Crystal as young adults, on their wedding day. All of these mementos were like talismans to conjure up the magic of Crystal Brook.

She carefully lay down on the dirty wood and closed her eyes. She imagined this was what meditating was. Taking in a sharp breath of air, she smelled a hint of eucalyptus from the Jefferson's garden next door.

"Crystal, Crystal."

Now she looked to her side and saw young Brook sitting next to her. She was back in her youthful and skinny body.

"What do you think is happening?"

He was referring to the sounds of a distant argument. She shrugged, unsure. She didn't have an answer. That year her parents divorced. Crystal's mother abandoned her for Mr. Hugo, a car salesman, who sold Crystal's family their station wagon. Brook's mom became like a surrogate mother to young Crystal, but her dad was never the same after that, except with his morning bourbon. Little Crystal remained stoic sitting there, side by side with Brook, as the shouting became an incessant car alarm, impossible to ignore. Brook placed his hand on hers. He spoke slowly, as English was still coming to him in fragments. "Let's go somewhere?"

"And where would we go?" she snapped.

"An exciting place where we have powers!" His hair flew over his eyes.

"And you and I are king and queen. I have a sword, you, a crown … " and so he trailed off. She let his words wash over her, like a cool breeze. She stopped him to add, "and there has to be water. Mom never wanted me to have a swimming pool. Ooh, and a castle befitting a queen." Like big blue discs, her eyes lit up, allowing Brook to take her to a fantasy world.

There's no fighting in the land. And candy grew on trees. People could fly. Animals talked. Their favorite animal was a bluebird, which greeted them with jokes during

breakfast. A typical day at court meant playing go fish all day. And before she knew it, the loneliness she felt vanished.

She closed her eyes again, happy, and began to check out until VROOM! It was the sound of the station wagon peeling out of the driveway, officiating the exit of Crystal's mom.

Every week for the next few years, these two best friends came to Crystal Brook and escaped into secret adventures. In fourth grade Brook and Crystal saw the court doctor when she broke her ankle roller skating. In fifth grade Brook took Crystal to a jousting tournament on her birthday. During their elementary school graduation they fought and won an epic battle against an evil invader. No matter what was happening, Crystal admired Brook's ability to make believe.

During her junior high school years, Crystal Brook became a long forgotten dream. Brook's mom got a job in California and the two friends kept in touch on and off over the years. During their last years in high school, they stopped talking. Crystal had a boyfriend and Brook took an extra job when his mother had cancer and needed extra money around the house. According to Crystal, life ceased to have any room for Crystal Brook anymore.

Then, adulthood inevitably came. Brook went to a college in California to stay near his mother. Crystal went to school in New York with her boyfriend, who kissed another girl during her birthday party. Typical. No longer able to face New York and feeling lost in life,

Crystal moved out to California. She toyed with the idea of being an actress. During a play reading, Crystal realized she wanted to create worlds rather than interpret someone else's vision. She enrolled in college in California as an English major. She wanted to write.

So-called serendipity brought Crystal and Brook together again in a seminar class. Crystal explained that her dad was doing better. He lived in New Haven and Brook's mother survived her fight with breast cancer. Brook came a long way from being the shy boy she remembered. He had tattoos on his arms, rode a motorcycle, quoted Oscar Wilde, and could make his own whiskey. He wanted to backpack through Southeast Asia, eat poisonous fish in Japan, or run with the bulls in Spain. Crystal was the same girl, who didn't know that the shirt she wore brought out the blue in her eyes and never stopped thinking about how her mom left her.

They bonded over new restaurants in their college town, proofed each other's essays before turning them in or going on spring break together. One day, during one of their dinners and after a few glasses of sangria, she kissed him. She had never made the first move before with a guy. He was a world of chances for her—ways for her to get out of her own shell, now the reversal of their beginning so many years ago in Crystal Brook.

Like a snake, she shed a layer of skin every time she was with him. He was the only one she confided to about her mom's recent attempts to contact her. She cursed out loud and openly cried about her mom. She admitted she couldn't find herself forgiving her dad for his past drinking. She got her first tattoo in a shady part of town. She overcame her fear of heights rock climbing. Because she was with her best friend, Crystal welcomed the simultaneous thrill and fear of shedding her little kid floaties and diving headfirst into the deep end.

Then one day, during a camping trip, she wondered how he felt.

"I don't know. No matter how crazy I get, you're about what's happening here around me," Brook paused, thinking. It made sense; she kidded that perhaps her problems were dragging him depressingly back down to earth. He added, "You bring me down to Earth. But it's good." What a sap, Crystal said out loud jokingly and she added he always talked about doing things that seem so out there, *so different*. Brook replied he likes to talk about the serious things, even his worries with paying back student loans someday, or hoping his mom didn't have cancer again. Sensing the gravity the conversation had taken, he gave her a devilish grin and nudged, "Have you ever been skinny dipping?"

Crystal could only laugh at his suggestions, which were 100% serious, 100% of the time. "I'll go, if you go first." She took off her shirt, exposing her neon pink bra and kissed him deeply. "You're bad for me." She took off her shoes and continued, "I'll race ya'." She sprinted first. He ran after her. They disappeared down the dirt path leading to the lake, like flies buzzing away in the distance.

Crystal opened her eyes again in the tree house now—years of memories engulfing her today on the 22nd of July, her wedding anniversary. She needed air. She found a beetle crawling up her arm and gently flicked it off. Sitting up, she eyed the corner of the tree house where Brook had proposed to her nearly five years ago. She could feel her eyes wet.

"What the hell?"

Crystal quickly gathered her things at the sound of a voice she recognized. It was the Mathesons, the family who purchased this house. She and Brook sold the house to pay for Brook's chemotherapy and medical bills. This was when she put on 15 pounds while he lost 15, and she had shaved her head while he lost his hair. They were together, always.

Crystal stuffed everything in her bag and WHOOSH! The urn fell over: half of Brook and broken blue porcelain pieces were on the floor. Literally, parts of him were slipping away through the slits between the wood. Crystal gave up trying to gather the ashes. She laughed involuntarily, saddened by this sight but she wasn't crying anymore and then she took a second to evenly spread him around.

As she climbed down the tree, she met Mr. Matheson, an austere Boston Brahmin, whose gaze burned a hole through her. She must have looked like a wild animal to him. "You can't come in here like this. This is private property." He held up his phone to call the police. If there was a hint of sympathy in him, he certainly wasn't showing it.

Crystal slowed down. "Please."

Mr. Matheson was dialing already and in a flash, she launched herself towards him and knocked his phone down in the fall, cracking its touchscreen on the cement. Hopefully Mr. Matheson regretted pouring cement over the garden, thought Crystal.

"Sorry! I'm terribly sorry." She sort of wasn't.

She ran through the side entrance of the garden and landed on the lawn like a cat on its feet after a jump. A swarm of fireflies now buzzed in the twilight. Only she didn't have time to admire this view, as the sprinklers sputtered around her, right on cue. Great. She reached her car and could still hear the incoherent shouts of Mr. Matheson, who raced out after her, panting and flailing his old noodle arms about.

Crystal turned the key in the ignition and her lips curled up. She took one fleeting glance back at the house, where the tree house peeked out over the top of the chimney and the amber sunset rimmed around it. Brook always had a way of turning everything into something grand. Part of her always thought she needed him to make life less dull, but now she realized the memory of him was important too. He will always be a part of her, inspiring her to color outside the lines. She had the inner strength now to create her own adventures. And with that epiphany, Crystal sped away from Crystal Brook.

About The Author

Jeane Wong is a Los Angeles native and UCLA alum. She is an alumni of the Producer's Guild Workshop and the Nickelodeon Writer's Workshop. And she has placed as a semifinalist in both the ABC Disney Writing Program and Larry Brody's TVWriter.com Contest. Currently, she co-authors the digital *The Vampire Diaries* comics for D.C. Comics and works on the show *White Collar*.

Follow her on Twitter: @jeanedevivr

About the Lupus Foundation of America, Inc.

T he Lupus Foundation of America is the only national force devoted to solving the mystery of lupus, one of the world's cruelest, most unpredictable, and devastating diseases, while giving caring support to those who suffer from its brutal impact.

Through a comprehensive program of research, education, and advocacy, we lead the fight to improve the quality of life for all people affected by lupus.

Visit **www.lupus.org** to join the fight and learn more.